THE
ERRORS
OF
YOUNG TJAŽ

THE
ERRORS
OF
YOUNG TJAŽ

by

Florjan Lipuš

Translated by
Michael Biggins

DALKEY ARCHIVE PRESS
CHAMPAIGN / LONDON / DUBLIN

Originally published in Slovenian as *Zmote dijaka Tjaža* by
Založba Obzorja, Maribor, 1972

Library of Congress Cataloging-in-Publication Data

Lipuš, Florjan, 1937-
[Zmote dijaka Tjaza. English]
The errors of Young Tjaz / Florjan Lipus ; Translated by Michael Biggins. -- First Edition.
pages cm
"Originally published in Slovenian as Zmote dijaka Tjaza by Zalozba Obzorja, Maribor, 1972."
ISBN 978-1-56478-908-2 (alk. paper)
I. Biggins, Michael, translator. II. Title.
PG1919.22.I63Z413 2013
891.8'435--dc23
                    2013022252

Partially funded by a grant from the Illinois Arts Council, a state agency

In cooperation with Slovene Writers' Association—Litteræ Slovenicæ Series

This project has been funded with support from the European Commission.
This publication reflects the views only of the author, and the Commission cannot be held
responsible for any use which may be made of the information contained therein.

This work has been published with the support of the Trubar Foundation, located at the
Slovene Writers' Association, Ljubljana, Slovenia.

This translation has been financially supported by the Slovenian Book Agency.

www.dalkeyarchive.com
Cover: design and composition by Mikhail Iliatov
Printed on permanent/durable acid-free paper

CONTENTS

I.

A CHAPTER ABOUT
WEEDS

The time has come for you to walk through the village. All vacation long you haven't walked through it in as big a way as you do today. It's not your native village—where you'd never permit yourself this kind of presumption—but the one located between the railway station and your family's house, and that doesn't mean much, barely more than that you've consented to its being there, even though it's in your way when you walk to the station. When you pass through it from one direction or the other—it doesn't matter which—you whistle, you make a point of puckering your lips and whistling in every direction, it's your password to the locals, it's how you recognize your village and distinguish it from other villages, it's how it glints in your memory. You learned to whistle precisely on account of your village, this random jumble of musty buildings, even though there are thousands like it, you whistle your way through your village alone, it's nothing less than it deserves for being responsible for your even learning to whistle at all, you didn't used to show any predilection for it, that's all its doing, it's given you plenty of time and space to practice, you've had limitless opportunities to whistle and pucker your lips till they produced sound, here whistling lifts you up and makes some sense, here one whistle finds support in another, your particular whistle practically buries the villagers, clobbers them with its clots of sound, you've become a good whistler and they've pricked up their ears, you've whistled up a name for yourself. When you walk through the village you split it in two, producing a left piece and a right piece, you pick up the sound of the villagers in the left piece and the villagers in the right piece, you sort out your villagers to the left and the right and you glance first in one direction, then in the other, you pick out your people to the right and the left and give them a chance to greet you, enabling, in other words, their first sentence of the day, the chance to put their first subject and predicate into play, which almost always has to do with the weather, thanks to you they notice the state of the weather on still empty stomachs, they force you to join them in fretting over fair or rainy weather, you've acquired some real weather smarts, constant experience and practice have honed your ear, regular skirmishes with the villagers have formed you into a formidable forecaster. Along the way hens cluck, cows low, or a dog yips, you rely on dogs, they've always been on your side. The first task awaiting the village after you board the train is to reunite the dismembered village, they tend to this as soon as you're gone, the village comes to life, they converge from all sides wherever they can, they're not picky when it comes to that, and it's urgent, besides, because the village has been dismembered and laid to waste, they gather in doorways, midway between neighbors, at crossroads, on this or that side of wooden slab fences or wherever, in matters like these they're really not picky or petty, they never have been and there's no need, anyplace is fine to exchange a few words, any old place will do for them to put heads together and confirm the time of your departure, because that's where you're headed, you're off to the station, so it's your own fault, they've got something up their sleeves, one thing today and something else the next, they're damn precise when it suits them, they count up how many times you've used the word ass instead of rear or bottom, they're convinced that ass is ugly but rear and bottom are all right, they divide the villagers into two social classes, one class with rears and bottoms and the other with asses, and you can guess which class they've put you in as you head for the train, it's come to light, it's coming to light, then disappears in the night, runs through the night, and then, on the other side, comes to light once again, one bit of news collides with another, they wring them out and pair up while wringing them out, their heads come together for one last squeeze, their hands can't squeeze any tighter, their heads can't come any closer, the couplings last until they're exhausted. In this sense you aren't actually sitting on the train, even though you've boarded it in the meantime, instead you're stuck in your villagers' maws, become the cause of these couplings. Even though they're not yours and you're not theirs, they are yours and you are theirs, because they've adopted you as their own, they don't have any other, they've taken pity on you, you'll do in a pinch, you're fine and you've proven to be useful, it's enough that you go whistling through their village, you've repeated your route so many times and diced their village to bits, so minutely have you scuffed your way down their asphalt roads and their dusty paths that they've taken you for their own. Now you're theirs, they worry about you and you're in their hearts, they haven't yet settled on what you'll become, definitely something, but exactly what still isn't quite clear, you'll become what you can, whenever you can, this perhaps, for sure not that, maybe this, and that if things work out, a boss if nothing gets in the way, some sort of boss and it's not clear what kind, but that doesn't matter, the main thing is you won't have to grind away like the villagers do, they've marked you for bosshood and that sticks to you now, it won't ever leave you, you owe it to them, this much you know, you're the chosen one and they've opened the whole world to you because you walk through their village on the way to vacation and then back from vacation to catch the train. You've grazed past the yellowed corners of houses, shacks, and barns that dogs have sprayed with their juice, you've walked past their houses and cut through many a yard, many a crack in a door has secretly squeaked open, many a curtain has silently come to life as you've passed by, you've had power over the cracks and the curtains and the lurking eyes, it's felt like an honor, so you haven't walked through the village in a big way without a good reason. The train chugs its way here, assaults the station, and marks the end of a period of your boarding school days, you've never come so much to life as you have this year, something is brewing inside you, unsuspected things are hatching their plots, this vacation is behind you,

you expanded your lungs in its air, its sun crashed into your face, you rowed your way into your first loves, you uprooted your senses and submerged them in moments now unforgettable. You brought certain vacation instructions with you from the boarding school, you'd been brought together in the assembly hall in your Sunday suits and your holiday shoes, there you were showered with precepts and don'ts, advice, warnings, recommendations, do this, don't do that, you must, you must not, on account of these or those reasons, your heads swarmed with prophylaxis, your chests grew heavy and dark. You weren't there, you fended off the wave of poison-tipped arrows, at the right moment you tucked in your tail and shook off the leash, sneaking into the room upstairs where the typewriter welcomed you, that flickering rattle of letters, you often retreated to it, it helped you out of more than one fix. What sort of texts Tjaž first entrusted to the typewriter and how he found his way into that world in the first place is no longer knowable, only a handful of letters from that time attesting to the typewriter exist. He managed to conceal this activity all those years without ever being found out, there were times when he regularly wrote with it, more or less following a set schedule, on Sundays for instance during the time set for group walks, on Saturdays during afternoon devotions, during catechism or confession or other occasions. Whether or not the use of typewriters was forbidden and punishable Tjaž didn't really even know, the house rules were mysteriously silent about it. When for instance they prayed aloud in church for the nations of the world to shake off the communist yoke and for success in shoving some deliciously wrapped Christian candy through some hole in the iron curtain, Tjaž would be hunting letters on his keyboard, candy like that leaves a taste behind that even you haven't got rid of yet, it still creeps through your mouth, even though you long since swallowed, digested, and shat it out. Once you infringed on this or that house rule and the prefect called you into his office so the two of you could discuss it alone and at length, complete with all the commas and periods, so to speak, but you didn't show up at the appointed time, you declined the invitation, you wouldn't give them a chance to show you their kindness and shine their magnanimity on you: this time you're forgiven, we'll forget all about it, you'll be spared any punishment, but next time watch yourself, make sure you resist temptation and stay out of mischief. You were nowhere near them, they couldn't bestow upon you what they'd prepared, what they had ready at hand and only needed to reach out and secretly pinch off a bit of, just for you, and daub into your lap, the others don't need to know, the whole business could have been put to rest, everyone could have felt good about it, the whole house would have learned of the nobility of the good fathers in letting Tjaž off without any punishment, this time, but next time probably not, everyone would be satisfied and everyone would have found succor, everyone would be able to glow in Christian fulfillment and sweat in self-satisfaction, if only Tjaž had accepted the offer, but Tjaž didn't accept, he didn't let them take him by the arm and drag him by a leash at the same time. While the nations of the world were trying to shake off the yoke of communism and examining options for getting candies over to the other side, while something was already beginning to move behind the iron curtain thanks to the candy-smell drifting across, Tjaž was serenely banging the keys, and on another occasion communism gave way to more immediate household concerns, and for that purpose litanies, of the Loreto sort, I believe, started to bloom throughout the church, and it started to rain virgins and queens so heavily it was a joy to behold, and that's when the keys would thrash at the ark of the covenant and the cup of the eucharist, that's when they banged at the house of gold and the gates of heaven, and the ivory tower collapsed on the tower of David, and the keys gushed at the flower of mystery and the morning star, in short, it was the dawning of our moment of glee but of hard times for the saints and apostles whenever Tjaž would harness his typewriter, no wonder then if they preferred not to poke into any private affairs and listen to this and listen to that or spread god knows what around, they didn't go getting tangled up in the grousing of god's own people, so the treasures of paradise were left untouched, but to make up for this they squandered that many more words in the fes-

tive, pre-vacation assembly hall, lavishing so much advice and so
many detailed warnings on the students that it really got their juices
going. The director was in a bad mood that day, the vacation had
him worried, he measured leisure out to his wards with such caution, drizzling vacation on them only gradually, hesitant to accede
to this demand for a break and fighting a mental battle with himself, because in each of his wards both evil and good longed for a
change and demanded fresh air, that much was palpable, they could
realize themselves in such conditions that much more easily. At their
homes everything still remained in its place, as before, they would
never, let's say, change an office into a cupboard or a library into a
bedroom, but they wouldn't have had to go that far, it would have
sufficed for them just to rearrange the furniture a bit, move something here, adjust something there, turn something around, chan-
nel life into some other space, water onto some other mill, a little
change like that would have softened many a fall and balanced out
many a blinkered view. Tjaž's own people back home were no different in that respect, nothing changed, the kitchen kept being a kitch-
en, the bedroom stayed the old bedroom, the shed was unremit-
tingly a shed, the cellar a cellar, the closet a closet, they were no
different from the bedroom, kitchen, shed, and cellar of, say, fifty
years ago, everything had its fixed place like the words in the our
father, you couldn't switch them with others, turn them around or
leave them out if you wanted, or they'd accuse you of heresy. Only
Tjaž switched his room around to his heart's content, the wardrobe
and the desk and the bed got no peace from him, one day he'd exile
the desk to the window and the bed to the door, the next day he'd
burden the long wall with the wardrobe, and on the day after that
he'd draw all of the furniture into a circle along the next wall, and
so forth, in short, he'd give his room a good shuffling and dusting.
That's not the only thing you take back to school from vacation,
your dowry is much bigger than that, you're full of experiences,
standing upright like a sack of potatoes, you've grazed your fill on
vacation goodies and lowered your head into unaccustomedly fresh
fodder, now you're heading back to account for how you invested all

the advice, the instructions and precepts, how they bore fruit and even now you can hear the stool pigeons whistle their disapproval, some of which has found its way into the priest's report on your vacation comportment, that's nothing to worry about, the priest likes you and takes your side, no, the worst is what you nurture inside you, or, rather, more wicked than worst. Your visit to the priest and his flock of benefactresses comes off well, you showed them your report card and explained your marks, you put on a show and lamented your mistakes and behold, all were relieved, it helped, it'll come in handy and you already know what you're going to buy, you honestly think when you thank him for it it comes from the heart, this is all the currency you have left that counts for anything. You blew the bulk of your vacation on everyday things, but they couldn't persuade you to fritter your old nag of a life away on holy minutiae, it's not some old rope, you lived and allowed life to live inside you and out of you, you were there so to speak at the birth of a philodendron leaf, you were attentively there with your bow stretched taut, still you didn't pull its individual fibers by the ears, the tongs, let's say, relaxing, the plucking and unrolling, the work, what work, the convulsions of its birthing muscles sailed right past you, you didn't waste the tiniest thought on such things, you lived the philodendron leaf, you live it even now, until some day you die it, you've taken life as it's come, and that's all. It hasn't been much, what you've lived, but it's been, you've left a piece here, a piece there, it's dried up on you and blown to bits, even that has happened, and you've struggled to assemble the remaining staves into a usable vessel. Once you approached the village church, which you'd pass on the way to the train station. It strutted atop the hillside, deliberately at the highest point if not an inch higher, there was no getting it higher than that, the village houses jostled humbly at its foot, they turned on their chimneys and sent clots of black cream billowing up under its nose, crops arrayed themselves over the distant fields, the pastures and cabbage patches rushed with their tithe. He shot it from two or three sides, studied its style, and let its churchly pressure work on his stomach's digestive acids. A girl was weeding in the cemetery, probably the sexton's daughter or ward—judging from her clothes more ward than daughter, or from her face more daughter than ward—she crouched by the wall in a genuine weeder's crouch, her knees under her chin, her hands thrust in the dirt, her eyes following her hands. She weeded, distinguishing one weed from another, separating the weeds from the mounds, the stones from the sand, crosses from tares, markers from lanterns, plantings from paths. Tjaž was transfixed by her full, powerful movements, defined cheeks, ponytail, first budding of breasts, darting hands, and busy fingers, a girl of tall, Gothic stature. Whether it was god's will or wasn't god's will, god only knows, Tjaž began to look at her from the bottom instead of the top, and in doing this he was already aware of his error. A boarding school student categorically looks at a woman from the top, and only if his eyes lead him astray and a woman's other regions unavoidably offer themselves, for instance the mid-, lower, or, god only forbid, bottom parts, then he is not to force his eyes away, but to look at all regions in equal measure and with equal intensity, and if it is possible, he is to focus his eyes on a safe, reliable area, he is to seek out the calm eye of the storm, so to speak, and hold out there for as long as the vision lasts, and from there he is to work his eyes centrifugally out and look for an exit, he is to dip systematically askance, down and across until he takes in all of the parts, taking care to do justice to each separate part, devoting equal attention to each, his looks are all to be equal regardless of where they linger, for all parts of the human body are equal and this is particularly true of the female body. Tjaž gave his eyes free rein, and too much freedom is never a good thing, they chose at their will, excluding too much here, focusing too much there, they wouldn't make do with the global, collective impression that the weeder's body imparted, they permitted themselves too much of certain individual parts, too much detail, they splintered too selectively, they marked trunks for removal, they shouldn't have circled and lingered on each petty thing, that's what they shouldn't have done, eyes grow petty if you don't rein them in. Tjaž changed the purpose of his appearance here, he dismissed his interest in the church and instead of the church began collecting details about the girl, shooting her from a distance, then closer up, from this or that side, he wound ahead on the roll in order to separate these, the girl from the churchyard walls of his earlier photos, the film crackled as it captured its prey, the crunching of the camera roused the weeder from her work, she raised her shapely body and at that point Tjaž sinned once again, he crouched down beside her in the midst of the weeds, not too close, but also not so far that she couldn't hear him, this was enough for a start, it was still too soon for anything physical. He started pulling up weeds by the roots, they didn't talk much, he asked questions more than spoke, she was silent more than she answered, they weeded the graves, her sickle cut the weeds to the quick, their fingers strangled their tiny stalks, the little roots writhing in revolt and spraying his and her fingers with their vile sap, but none of that was of any avail, they rooted them all up one after the other nonetheless and tossed them onto the compost, refusing them earth, denying them water, nutrients, and earth, banishing their verdant desire, sapping, so to speak, the last bit of their will to live. The work was finished, bits of dirt clung to his and her fingers, he could feel its curative, clinging touch, the rancid scents of the weed roots wrinkled the skin and dirt dug into the furrows, he lifted his fingers to his nose and sniffed, so that's how it smells, slightly different from the dirt back home, it smells of vinegar, the dirt from the field at home tended toward bitter, and he also sniffed at the grass. The dirt dried quickly on his warm hands, he scraped it out of the furrows and picked his fingers clean as whole layers dropped off, he also felt his scab, while trying to harness the horse he had injured his hand, the blood had dried and since then the scab never occurred to him, but now he had scraped it again and blood seeped from the wound, though it caused him no pain, the drops of blood only tickled a bit and their lazy slide did his skin good, the blood mixed in with the dirt, he wasn't paying attention to this, he was heading home with his mind on the girl weeding, he hadn't studied the church, he would next time, and anyway he had caught it on film and could study it at home, he thought about how much time would have to pass before the weeds grew back and would have to be pulled out again, that's when the village church that he passed on the way to the station would awaken in him again, its frescoes, inscriptions on tombstones, the ossuary and saints, and that would be another chance, and a lucky coincidence would allow him to repeat that fateful afternoon and, what's more, to escalate the encounter and go one step further, the weeding would make it that much easier. You won't have to wait for the weeds to grow back, you can go there anytime, fortunately you're not dependent on the growth of the weeds, you've sniffed honey, you're onto its track, and you haven't let it out of your sight, you got to the bottom of things, you investigated and found out that your chosen one didn't just weed graves but tended cows too, this saves you and relieves your pain. She was tending cows by the river, the sexton's three dappled calves, just a shade scrawnier than the priest's, but otherwise bright-horned and dark-scowled, they knew him already and that's why, as he approached, they only lifted their heads and sank them right back down into the grass, yielding out of their own instincts and relinquishing the field of battle to him, they let him go about his affairs without any witnesses and, indeed, indulge himself. He sat down beside her, this time much closer. When he began to kiss her on the neck, along the edge of her hairline, and, to the extent it was possible, under the collar of her dress, it was clear that the boarding school's quota had once again been overstepped, and this time far overstepped, so far that there was no going back, but it had been overstepped long ago, at least when together they had taken up arms against the weeds, wreaking such devastation on them, far more than had been planned for that afternoon, but at this point that was no longer decisive. When his fingers lingered someplace a little farther and carried out a small experiment, the tiniest, most innocent little experiment, experimenting with this and experimenting with that, as befits this sort of thing, and finally managed to introduce some method into the whole business, for instance by starting to stroke systematically, one thing at a time, but each thing from its extremity, as is the general practice in these cases, and then, as is only fitting if a person is healthy, it wasn't long till the norm burst with a loud twang and in wide arcs its last parts went flying, he was on the verge of pursuing this thing to the end, but at that point certain reservations appeared, this far and no farther, not a pinch more, a good boarding school student knows his boundaries and doesn't just let caution fly to the wind. When it gushed out, he was afraid she might feel the dampness through her dress and he didn't want her to notice he was soggy. A week later they would meet up again and that time it would be different, that time he would be bold and do it properly. The voices of shepherds, those resentful roosters, stretched all along the far side of the river, and their whooping suggested the pair had been noticed, but that was no problem. They baked apples and roasted potatoes and they craned their necks in the process, sure, but the seed of the ferns didn't slide into their pockets, if you know what I mean, midsummer night hadn't dawned for them, they were no match for Peter Klepec, they couldn't even see him, midsummer night belonged to Tjaž. The moon pauses in the sky on its way to far-off lands, you can see it at every step, first it goes backward, then it goes forward, whichever is easier and wherever the path is clear, and you don't even notice it's in a hurry to get, say, to Australia or South Tyrol, you've left it in peace where it was, it traversed half the globe and you didn't grimace, it traverses the whole globe and you don't grimace, you're busy with love, you're tending your needs, curing your aches as best you can, one way today, another tomorrow, less well one day, better the next. The vacation races to its end, the last days bunch up in front of you, you say good-bye, drinking late into the night, normally you don't drink, but today you drink by way of exception, and you do it up right, but normally you really aren't like this, today you drink enough for you to send a stone flying through space, you come by this thanks to your father, it clings to you from your father, you've inherited his traits, you're becoming like him, you don't know what to do with your strength so you vest it in this stone, your stone falters as it makes its way over the little heads and fat asses worshiping at the tavern, you serve them up your stone, they can see from its course that a drunken hand threw it, and that's why the diners and drinkers retract their heads into their shoulders, little heads colliding with fat asses and fat asses colliding with little heads, a stone is a stone and there's never any knowing what its intentions might be, the diners and drinkers retract their ass-like heads from its flight path, just to be safe, because you never know, they have to be ready and reckon with any eventuality, a stone isn't just straw or a word, you're never safe from it, it passes a hair's breadth over their heads, indeed ruffling the few fine hairs on their skulls, where you can see the hooklike seams of their skull bones, it cleaves the air with its hatchets, a little hatchet like this does a nice little job of sniffing out human blood, of disrupting the columns of cigarette smoke, it races past the arc lights that hang over outspread newspapers and illuminate little scandals, that hung over outspread newspapers and illuminated little scandals, that will no longer hang over outspread newspapers and illuminate little scandals, there won't be any more need, the stone creeps along over there, nice and slow, it's in no hurry, inch by inch, it undertakes its mission with a great deal of care, these are precious moments that you sip down into the depths of your belly, because you're this stone's author, you'll live off these rations for a number of years, your stone has seen everything and there's no job it wouldn't be up to, that's your stone for you, any instant it's going to hit its target toward the front, way toward the front, where there's maybe a wall made of bamboo or plywood, that kind is cheaper, or maybe it's just a plain wall without any bamboo or plywood, even that kind will do in a pinch, in winter this part of the tavern is closed, maybe an aquarium, better not an aquarium, better a bull or a tree, those are your specialty, everybody pick out a bull and everybody pick out a tree, whichever you prefer, or if you'd rather go for the back of some guest and the head of the pretty barmaid who serves up whatever her customers order, then them, let's go for those two, that would be best, there it would hit and drill a hole or create a dent, in other words accomplish its task, what a shame, a dent or a hole in the customer's back or the pretty barmaid's head, she doesn't have to be your sweetheart, who says so, you shower your joy on each one alike. You wasted quite enough time finding a girl, and not just any kind, but the kind suited to you, but of these any will do, you start trailing her, you follow behind her, stay on her trail, you have the same path ahead of you as she does, even though you don't know it, her path and yours, you lift your feet high so you don't shuffle and give yourself away, you can never step too high, but too low is a constant risk, you don't like for them to notice you too soon, you're on her heels or you pass her and approach her head on, you need a certain distance and a certain angle of vision to masturbate, some boys masturbate as they walk, others stop and masturbate standing or hide behind a chestnut tree, it varies from one student to the next, you have to understand, not all boarding school students are created alike or are equally demanding, one is like this, the other's like that, and even where it comes to a particular individual, he isn't always in the same mood, one day he'll prefer one method and another the next. But to hell with their alleyway methods, if that from-a-distance method satisfies them, they're welcome to it, their scrotums will all go sour and there'll be no sap running there. You've skewered your hen, that sets you apart from them, even if you did pick her out in the weeds, you tend to her at night, you squander the whole night in her nest, warming your bones, you take your time, you've just about run the month out, traveling a long time till finally arriving, you've knocked and the door has opened. On your way back, the grass bows down to you, the weeds flutter from the furrows and borders, a tree has planted its outstretched legs, it smells of dew, flowers blossom, the chirping of birds fills the crotches of trees, sap flows through them, the first sunlight searing their crowns. You proudly make your way through the village and past homesteads where well-rested people are retreating from night, barely has the sun twitched its rabbit muzzle over the horizon, and barely has dawn started draping the trees with bugs and birds and squirrels and splashed dew out onto the meadows, your villagers are Mary's own people, they're so good and hardworking. You're a witness to how they tame the morning light, their lungs pecking at the fresh air. Field and garden call and the meadow can't stand without them, the tools come to life, cattle stretch in the barn, fences straighten out of the glens and send shoots through the pastures, grain outgrows itself, the borders between fields come to life, field gates go into action, the first vehicles rumble down the paths, from the far side of the forest a windstorm sets out to butt into the hay-laden ricks, calluses get ground down off of hands. You know what it means when first thing in the morning all through the village fathers appear at their children's bedsides, gruesome scenes. The earth demands its share and the people measure it out, some in a miserly way, others with abandon, but one way or the other all of them measure it out, what good is resisting, for the sake of his daily bread each one of them submits to the pressure and contributes his share, the earth is the earth and only gives if it gets. This is when you make your way through the village and while walking you think about one thing and another, a few things you work out, your eyes are still dreaming, you leave them to their fun and depend on your feet, which know the way by heart, you grind through experiences of the night barely past, while morning rises beneath your feet and the early crows squawk you up into the sky, taking your weight, so you walk lightly. In all of the faces you make out a bit of her face, behind every body there hides a bit of her body, and every puddle reflects a bit of her stream. Then you veer off of the road, you push uphill toward the family house, because the sun is making quick progress and already shining on all the mountains and peaks, it's time for you to speed up. The vacation inclines toward its close, you can't hold back its sunset, you manage to knock a few last morsels off of it and no more, you buzz around for the last several days, several nights you go to say good-bye, one night more thoroughly, the next just in passing, the first is exhausting, the other exhilarating, you put body and soul together, you're getting ready for school, because you know it's ready for you, they've warned it about you, it's keeping track of you, informed and expectant, but this union of body and soul isn't something you can keep up. Once, when you were little, you took food out to your father where he was staying in a woodsman's hut, using words and hand

gestures your father described the route, where you would have to
veer off and when you would have turn this way and when that way.
Your father was never exactly a master storyteller, it was hard for
him to explain things to you, and you never knew how to bridge the
empty spaces and fill in the gaps in what your father said. No wonder you took a wrong turn and couldn't find your father or the hut,
you got lost in the forest, you ran out of path, and you couldn't hear
the woodsmen at work anymore, lynx-eyed you looked for a way
out, you rooted around, wandered blindly this way and that, cried
and cursed and pleaded until the mountaintops spun, you got dizzy
and the ground slipped away under your feet, you ran out of curse
words, got sick of pleading, and the food in your backpack intended
for your father got heavier and heavier and finally pushed you to the
ground. In utter distress you headed back downhill with the conviction that you would get revenge, even if you didn't know how or
when, perhaps in the far distant future, curdling in your heart. You
ran in the direction of the ridges that were only slowly bending toward the valley when you suddenly stopped, shocked. An abyss
yawned into you, its emptiness touching you to your core, and it
rocked in front of you, almost as if it were dancing. You've grown
since then and still before your eyes is that abyss as it rocks, knowing of nothing down below but sea, shore, harbors, tempests, is-
lands, tempests, harbors, shore, and sea, rocking and swaying, swaying and rocking, rocking, rocking, swaying, swaying. Some trees
shoot past, the train has scratched its way through the countryside,
the engine searching out stations, wagging its way in kangaroo leaps
past the mountains and into the vast plain.

2.

A CHAPTER ABOUT
SOME BUSINESS WITH SHOES

From the very start the boarding school failed to notice Tjaž's developmental backwardness. This shouldn't have been surprising, because the boy had anchored himself deeply in a mediocrity that gave the educators in charge no cause for concern. His intellectual abilities weren't threatening, his emotional capacity posed no danger to the school, he gave no evidence of any special gifts or inclinations, his childish body, slow in growing, was in nobody's way, and he showed no need to court the favor of those in charge. The usual extent of official attention was enough for him, and that's why he never tried to elbow his way into the center of his fellow students' attention or exaggerate his importance to those in charge. In short, they didn't discover him. Because he didn't draw attention to himself, they didn't look for any reason to worry about him more than they would about anyone else. They had been informed about his birth, parents, place of birth, citizenship, religion, mother tongue, prior education—no more than that was needed. His number had been sewn onto every last handkerchief so the nuns could distinguish his laundry from others' without any trouble. He was weighed twice a year, in spring and in fall. Whenever he stood on the scales in his underpants, they shamelessly assigned him far too little weight, and whenever they checked his body's height with the ruler, the same numbers kept getting squeezed out, so height and weight remained forever the same. Because the boy himself had nothing against the measures and weights and because he never fished for exceptions in other respects either, because he never forced his way into the limelight and didn't seem to consider his objectively deficient numbers a problem, they overlooked his scant physical failings and categorized his data as normal. Even so, it would be easy to imagine the boy at some point or another along the way making a point of his condition, but with so many charges in their care you can hardly expect them to waste time on every little detail. He didn't accuse them of any crimes, nor did he fault them for any transgressions, he didn't ball his fists, he made no threats or demands, if he had done that, it would have started worrying them a lot sooner, but as things were he took whenever they gave and he gave whenever they took, they had to be completely satisfied with him, he didn't make them do any work, they didn't have to engage his body or mind, he matured without their having any problems with him, he matured at his own expense, so to speak. So what could have raised him up, what invisible thing, imperceptible to the senses, could have given him away, when there weren't even any visible, noticeable, tangible signs? The school truly had no reason to doubt his ordinariness or assign him any more responsible, exalted role in the life of the school than he already had, his ordinariness suited them fine. He fought down his share of brown flour soup along with the others, and it denied his mouth any salty or sweet taste, or bitter or sour, its only virtue being that it filled your stomach. He was affected just the same as all the others one morning when the tinny clatter like the clatter of a huge metalworking shop was replaced by the scraping of porcelain mugs, when the flour soup was driven out by Postum, and metal by porcelain. How easy it is to overlook the way little details can make for a festive atmosphere. That change was truly worthy of a holiday and practically threw the whole dining room out of joint. If there was any day on the school calendar that deserved to be highlighted in red, then it was the day when they changed the utensils and kitchen cookware, dazzling the students' eyes with wonderment at this unexpected event. They licked the porcelain walls inside and out, and probably no saint ever took as much licking as the Postum-stained porcelain did in those days. Tjaž also lived through the time of brown flour soup and Postum, if not joyfully, then at least at peace with those in charge. Nothing in particular happened during those years, aside from the fact that no progress was made on his growth. There was other progress to be noted all up and down the line, life was getting better, and bread was allowing itself to be dunked for longer periods, whereas before it wouldn't even get thoroughly soaked through in some warm, porcelain bath before spoons had to go in for a rescue and deliver it as quickly as possible to post-war mouths for further processing. Everything was evolving for the better, only Tjaž stayed the same Tjaž, and if anything it seemed he was becoming slighter than ever, with neither the flour soup nor the Postum moving him off dead center. While others had mastered the art of holding a cup first with just one hand then at last with two fingers, he still needed to use both hands. He refused to open up, he simply couldn't get his body into bloom. How should this boy who'd already gotten a taste of quite a few holy missions, the priest harnessing him into various roles around the church and the rectory, a boy whose first Messianic convulsions had been triggered by peasant mulishness, who amid all the backwoods parochialism had become infected with incurable bullheadedness, a boy all of whose most fundamental assets had been eaten away by those around him, how was a boy like that, whose father had been so generous about laying into his back with the belt, how was a boy marked from an early age in this way supposed to grow at a normal rate? How was he supposed to care about developing from boy into man when he hadn't even begun living his earliest age, hadn't discovered it yet, hadn't been able to exhaust its possibilities? What could have sped up the activity of his growth hormones and who could have told him if his body was even still capable of producing them? But anybody who thought that the boarding school was a place of gluttony and idleness and licentiousness, or a refuge for the slow to develop, a sanatorium for crippled lives, was mistaken—far from it, something like that just couldn't be, one could not and must not be concerned with delays of a worldly nature, the boarding school is a place of work, a place of cultural betterment, obliged therefore to produce at any cost, even at the expense of ignoring physical needs, a new generation of the right mental cast, you're on your own for the physical stuff, eat and drink as best you can, in those matters you're free to be natural, there's no hero who doesn't pee when he poops, feed and sustain yourself so you can grow intellectually and develop spiritually according to *his* wisdom and plans, for he has great plans for you, he'll see to that, he has complete power over that and don't forget that these are the reasons you're in his ranks. This is important, there will be time and opportunities later for the physical needs. It starts early in the morning, they arrive from six or seven dorm rooms, washed, shod, their hair slicked down, outside the door they mix with the ones who sleep separately because they wet the bed, at the threshold they make two or three dots in the font and on their forehead with their right index fingers. Of course the first approach is very matter of fact, but it's necessary for the students to get their first look around, shake off their sleep, find their pews, leaf through three or four pages of icons in their prayer books until they reveal the saint of the day and get him used to the glaring light. Their virtues have not been sufficiently trained, the walls, the floor, the columns, and ceiling disgorge a chill all four seasons, so that the students warp in the cold like wood and their devotions blister. Still, if there was any earthly splinter at all still clinging to the communicants, it was certain to drop off during mass. Here the assembled company quivered oil-like in its prayers and seasickness assaulted the nave of the church, with the waves tossing it first toward one shore, then toward the other. A bell yipped with the ministrant's shining voice, then a deeper one yowled from the bell tower, as the assembled company responded, performing with all possible haste whatever the yipping and yowling commanded. The cogs of the ritual turned at full steam, but the students' devotion made only modest progress, and neither the boarding school nor its students had much to be proud of, all told. Waves of yawns were far too likely to pass through their ranks, fervor was doomed to failure as the boys became its mere instrument, nothing more than its milk cows, merely a means for piety to continue to be piety, for virtues to show they were virtues, just a condition of its further existence, because the life of the church requires a faithful people that submits and carries out its commands—in short, if there weren't a faithful people, the church would have no power and would have to consume itself in self-love and disillusionment, its presence in this world would be pointless, and just as without students the boarding school would have no power and no house rules, with no house rules there would be no piety, and with no piety there would be no church. During the reading Tjaž usually lost the last of his courage for tasting the delights of the beyond, no matter how hard he tried, the relief never lasted past the reading of the gospels. When the pre-Council Latin of the fat service book thundered through the church, fluttering bat-like around the basilica's pillars, darting over the boys' standard haircuts to the back pews, there to circle graciously over several glistening bald heads before bouncing off the slightly rusty iron fittings of the back door and pushing back down the center of the seasick nave to its source and collapsing, feckless, back into its nest, that's when Tjaž had exhausted his reserves, he had made his contribution, done his bit, there was nothing more to give. The end of mass every morning brought the biggest crush of all to the sleeping pews and new life to their lacquered, worm-eaten maple wood, about which no one knew if it was lacquered on account of the worms or worm-eaten on account of the lacquer. This maple wood had imprinted its own distinctive signs on each student's knees, elbows, and rear, the irreproducible signs of a boarding school. One moment the cement steps of the altar siphoned the pews to the front and then back to their places, the next they were kneeling and sticking their tongues out for the celebrant to weigh them liturgically down, one after the other, from the first to the last, with cleanliness radiant amid the pews hundreds of times over and immeasurable with even the most ponderous scales. Here a pew got up too soon, there one got up too late, on the right side a line formed too fast, while on the left the market day jostling was too slow to abate. How many curves and angles had to be closed, how many paths had to cross, how many steps had to be synchronized before the ecclesiastical geometry was satisfied. In front, the shoes, trouser legs, and cuffs of the communicants were on display for you to study in detail. There was no better occasion for this than communion, when the leg and foot of the kneeling communicant was motionlessly exposed to the acute eyes of those standing behind him, who not only evaluated the leather and soles and calculated longer or shorter remaining lives or played out some other game on them, who not only applied their dilettante expertise to the work of the shoemaker, working the awls, pulling the threads through the heels, and judging the heels stretched over the lasts, but sometimes, with a burst of laughter that they hastily sewed back shut, they kept watch over the birth of holes in many a stocking. On Sundays and holidays they would engage in spirited debates over shoe polish, then on weekdays doubt its very existence. Burdened down with new resolutions, they vied with each other in their zeal with the brush, which on the evening before had to lay into all the points where churchyard mud met worldly leather. That's what happened up front. All this time in the back somebody was constantly walking, somebody stood, or sat, or kneeled, or hung, or leaned, somebody stood up, genuflected, got in the way, sang, stayed silent, mumbled, repented, turned sour, somebody tripped on the steps, took short cuts, long cuts, or went in straight lines, somebody prayed through his teeth, or his beard, with his lips, through his nose, with his tongue, somebody spoke, expressed, accosted, persuaded, harangued, responded, and defended, somebody adjusted his face, deposited appropriate content into a handkerchief, rubbed an unbidden member against his trousers, somebody left the pew, kicked the pew, sawed the pew, blocked the pew, loved the pew, hated the pew, somebody returned to the pew, climbed into the pew, sailed into the pew, fled into the pew, bumped into the pew, somebody crawled over the pew, slept athwart the pew, pushed his way out of the pew, drummed on the pew, searched under the pew, kept watch over the pews, somebody added, multiplied, divided and subtracted the pews, somebody declined, thought, wanted, was a pew. Of all the boarding school students, Tjaž probably had the easiest time of all adapting to the house rules, which demanded unrelenting, bovine submission. Tjaž had managed to master this, having learned its basic rules at home from his father's foresightful belt, which had impressed the first laws of submission into his naked flesh in a highly memorable way. Presumably some well-couched words would have done just as well, but his father had never heard them himself, all his life he'd been used to flourishing the woodsman's hard tool in his hands, and so for his son's first life lesson the belt took precedence over the word. In spite of this, submission was very slow in penetrating his consciousness, and it never really got into his blood. While the others endured their first hot peppers, watched the jars of marmalade stack up, and forced down their ration of slops, these nuisances were spared Tjaž, for in this respect he had surpassed all of them, he always managed to duck and clench his teeth in the nick of time, it must be said that he was exceptionally mistrustful and cautious for his age, a model of obedience and attendance like few others, which was undoubtedly also the result of his small stature. He never forgot things, never got in the way, he never tested anyone's nerves, and usually took the smallest pieces on the platter for himself, even though he got no treats sent to him from home, he studied diligently and was a force to be reckoned with in church, divine service suited him well, he believed the homilies and the spiritual exhortations to the letter, inhaled the meaning of each dash, uncovered his head at each icon and cross and especially at test time gurgled up such pious sighs while standing in front of them that the school's mother superior would have been proud. At that point nobody could have imagined that, overnight, meek, humble Tjaž would turn into the worst scratcher that the nation had ever produced. True, he secretly rebelled against his father's arbitrary rules and had once, in an absolute emergency, pried the belt out of his father's hands, but it was while his father was writing a new rule on Tjaž's thighs that he succeeded at his first instinctive scratch, more or less as a last resort while being beaten. While Tjaž's head was clamped between his father's own thighs, he planted his claws into his father's arm until blood started glistening through the bristles, and as though thwacked by a branch piercing his skin, his father let go of his victim and roared as he would whenever he heaved an especially heavy log down the chute and into the valley, but by then Tjaž was long gone. It is, indeed, also true that that sort of rebellion is entirely in keeping with growing up, every healthy child rebels against his parents with greater or lesser success until he outgrows his whims and a more seemly relationship springs up between him and his superiors. Things took a slightly different turn with Tjaž, for whom there could be no thought of a seemly relationship, for he had tasted scratching, had experienced delight in the process, and had seen its unexpected effect when his father's bony thighs let go and stopped squeezing his throat and a trickle of blood started to work its way down the paternal arm. Escaping the woodsman's powerful grip meant something to the helpless rebel. When at the boarding school he took up scratching as a vocation, he'd already had his first experiences with the craft, his first practicum under his belt. Visions of certain targets swarmed before his eyes and he could clearly imagine his future pursuits. Even though at that point he had not yet taken to scratching regularly, only as needed, and although certain details, such as the time and place of the scratchings had not yet been worked out, his very first swipe still caused a great deal of commotion and just as much admiration. From the very beginning it was obvious that his scratches weren't just some romantic prank, much less lucky coincidences, but that here Tjaž's true calling was revealing itself and that it had to be taken with the utmost seriousness, the first instance of it having pointed unmistakably to that seriousness as it emerged from a family triviality to become a distinguished public fact—family settings always being the undignified things that they are and, this case being no exception, none too durable, Tjaž smashed his easily and his gift became known far and wide. That morning he was somewhat distracted, the assembled student body raced with the usual chaos through the divine service, while he found himself unable to engage with it. Prayers rattled solemnly out of throats and resonated droningly off the walls. It was one of those rare mornings when he didn't once open his mouth, and even his ears, which otherwise took note of every disharmony in church proceedings, weren't functioning that day. And so it's impossible to say if there was a hitch in the text that morning or if the front pews were once again ahead of the back by half a sentence. None of this mattered much anyway, because the students recited only short, readily comprehensible sentences of the sort common folk prefer, with the exception that the latter need to have them in large print, much in demand among those who complain of bad eyesight and have faulty pronunciation. That morning Tjaž just wasn't available for whatever was happening in the church, other needs preoccupied him, his religious feeling shamelessly left him in the lurch, his conscience as a good boarding school student didn't jolt him awake, a decision, a decision high up and far away from the everyday business of church was turning and spinning in his head, his brain was feverishly distributing the sparks it gave birth to and weighing their magnitude, thinking through his plan in its entirety and at last examining each of its phases separately. When the communion bell rang, his plan was launched into action. Footsteps clicked and clattered across the floor of the church, the priest whispering as he satisfied the tongues jutting out at him, as one by one the boys set forth toward the altar, presented their tongues, grazed, and then disengaged. Tjaž's pew jostled toward the front and then came to a stop, and the budding scratcher's heart leaped when he saw his victim in front of him, a fellow student who was warped like a wooden plank in the sun, his long legs thrust out behind him. Tjaž felt a fountain inside of himself that was like the one from his childhood, when his neck had been locked between his father's thighs and his father's law-giving belt assailed his limbs. Then his body had swum in the air and his arms waved several inches above the floor, a position from which he could see the back of his father's pitch-stained trousers from the knees down, his crudely tacked shoes and the wooden kitchen floor beneath them, which during the moments when his belt was having its way, lost all its feel of home and turned into the floor of some grim tavern. The boy was a bad swimmer, his spine twisted and wriggled too much, as though any instant it might go darting off in a wide arc god knows where, but the pain prepared Tjaž's hands for their work, they spoke to the fingers, awakened the nails, and through furious scratching the boy managed to stop the ritual his father had barely begun, and escape. Now the fountains were replenished, and they took hold of him, limbering him up for this new task. He gauged the distance, threw out his hook and line, and lo and behold, the shoe bit. First he untied the shoelaces and extracted them soundlessly through their eyes, then he attacked the soles and began to scratch the wooden tacks out of them, like a vulture he circled over the sole meat and milked it until the tacks trickled onto the floor. The scratcher was aware that he'd chosen good shoes that didn't already have two or three generations of boys on their backs, as Tjaž's did. By the final tacks, when the layers could smell liberation approaching, the leather began to peel away from the foot, and both shoes twisted and rippled and finally flopped apart, collapsing into pieces of various sizes and shapes with nothing left in them but the stitches and seams. Then, when he managed to scratch even those out, the weathered outer layers of leather separated from the softer intermediate and inner ones. Touching scenes offered themselves to Tjaž's analytical eyes: the leather yawned and stretched as if it had just awoken from a century-long sleep or were returning from its protracted captivity, its edges and curves groaning as they straightened back out. Tjaž had given the leather back its original shape from before it was fashioned, had restored it to freedom, delivered it from bondage—who could have kept a dry eye seeing how the leather soaked up all these kindnesses. Amid this warm, generous mood he almost forgot about the heels, he'd put them off till last, because he'd had doubts from the outset whether he was up to them, they were sewn, glued, compressed and nailed, and promised the most resistance of all, he was afraid the glue might cause trouble and limit his striking power. But when he cast out his hook, they readily seized it, and so he showed particular mercy in putting an end to both heels, the individual pieces coming apart forever. Tjaž's poor schoolmate soon discovered some anxious movement in the leather, though he was utterly incapable of understanding what it was about until he suddenly realized he was shoeless, in his stocking feet, his shoes having disintegrated into little bits. A spurt of common sense told him that no normal shoe could come to an end like that, and that extraordinary and incredible things were happening to him. Both of his shoes had given out simultaneously, at the same exact time, even though they had no reason to do so, collapsing into their component parts. Somebody had rooted each sole separately out of the leather without ruining or even slightly damaging the material, the culprit had disembodied the stubborn leather and disassembled the heels down to their thinnest inner layers, but the laboriousness of the dissection didn't show on them anywhere, he had managed to pluck the counters out of the heels and extract the thread without any damage, it was marvelous work, achieved through a succession of individual, equally adroit movements, and completed in no time at all, word started getting around, and everyone had to admire the technique and recognize the consummate craftsmanship, all the more so for its having been completed without any witnesses, nobody had seen or heard anything, even though the whole church had been there and at the fateful moments a few were within just inches of the unfortunate boy. Not until after the deed was done did the celebrant's whispered litany get stuck in his throat, the pews craned their necks right and left to look for the stocking footer, though he was right there in their midst, the heads compressed into bunches, the prefect up in the choir loft observing communion set his breviary aside and leaned over the railing, and all concentration was lost. But now was not the time to go digging through one's brain, trying to figure out how this could have happened, the boy was crushed by a single concern—how to vanish from the sight of so many eyes, how to slip away from their gaping mouths. If only the earth could have swallowed him up, but the ground of the school was too hard, and anyway the house rules left little leeway for that sort of exit. His face lost all color, because no matter what he might do, every step would only make things worse, he'd be stepping from the skillet into the fire, this was inevitable. But so far the affair was still bearable, there was still some chance it might turn out all right. He had put his shoes on an hour ago and worn them to church, he'd noticed nothing suspicious about them, they gave no sign that the stitches might give out and the shoes fall apart in the foreseeable future. If he wasn't mistaken, he had just bought them a month ago, so they should have been fine. Last night he had shined them and though, yes, maybe he had noticed a couple of tiny little cracks in the leather, they were otherwise impeccable, what harm could those barely visible little veins have done? He'd also applied plenty of polish to them, they were his favorite shoes to wear, they didn't pinch, they didn't flop on his feet, they adjusted to the contours of his skin and they were soft and quiet to walk in. There was nothing wrong with them, nothing at all, and he had knelt down for communion as he had countless times before, and suddenly his shoes were clawed apart, destroyed, crushed, without his having budged an inch or even feeling anything going on down there, nothing, they just collapsed into little pieces, that was all he could say about them. The remains lay on the floor, scattered this way and that, and the students kicked at them or picked them up and paraded them all around. Who would have thought an ordinary shoe was made of so many pieces. Something like this truly wasn't an everyday event, it was a calamity and it had deprived the boy of his shoes, he had to wait in his stocking feet for communion, that wasn't the terrible bit, up to this point it wasn't that bad, but how was he supposed to get up and go back to his pew, how far that was from here and not a single place to hide on the way, how bright this day was, how sunny, how generous the windows were this morning, how alone he was against his fellows filling the church. Should he make light of it, should he deliberately high-step his way down the aisle and draw the congregation's attention to his clan's knitting abilities, should he let everyone see the handiwork of his grandmother and aunt in wielding knitting needles, or should he take the event seriously and tragically, should he add a few tears and show his profound hurt, his disappointment, his bad luck? In all likelihood the unfortunate would have chosen one of these few possibilities, perhaps he would even have escaped from the vicious cycle,

FLORJAN LIPUŠ

if only time hadn't been so short. It was time to clear the stage, because the next line had already formed behind him. He was given no chance to perform, not even the tiniest little scene, hope had betrayed him, and just as he was, face pale as a ghost's, woolen-footed, unshod but wearing resplendently white everyday socks whose signature touch was a pronounced gray heel and a light green sole, just so, he fled from the altar back into his pew.

3.

A CHAPTER ABOUT
KILLING CROWS

The furniture in the attic room was warped, cracked, and rough-hewn and one had to be particularly careful when dealing with it. A table with curved thighs and two chairs demanded the central place in the room and got it, though that was up against the longer wall. The same wall yielded part of one corner to a couch. A wardrobe and a small table for toiletries shared space to the right and left of the door. The west wall clipped a few dozen square feet off of the room and with its odd angle gave it the shape of an irregular trapezoid. All that was left for the ceiling was a narrow, feebly painted strip. The walls that weren't covered with furniture offered space to a few flowerpots, some drawings demonstrating various techniques, still life paintings, and two or three specimens of feminine handicraft, with clippings from magazines and fashion journals to fill in the gaps. The angular attic wall lent some white to the other, colorfully bedecked and beposterered walls. Thanks to its abundant angularity the one wall's plaster had remained spotless through all the years, no picture frame nail had driven a hole through its little bubbles, no glue had latched its suckers onto it. No wonder that the plaster carefully, almost jealously guarded its whiteness, even threatened you with its virginity. There was no more sensible solution for this dead spot, this attic wall, than to locate a bed next to it. Not only the bed, nightstand attached, but all items of furniture here were arranged with practicality and efficiency in mind, but it had been impossible to force any particular appearance or sense of personality onto the room. Aside from her, nothing the room contained reminded him of her at all. The attic room was cheap and without any doubt deservedly so, but judging from the curtains and the dreary furniture it ought to have been free. It didn't surprise or disappoint Tjaž in the least, because he didn't have the slightest inkling what a girl's room should be like, right until that moment he hadn't been able to imagine it, it hadn't teased or incited his curiosity in the slightest, it struck him as a peripheral thing and until now he hadn't formed any opinion of his own about it. But now, as he crossed its threshold, he had to admit that the impression made by this room bothered him even more than Nini did herself. Perhaps this impression was due to the fact that it wasn't just any stranger, one of *them*, who lived in this room, but Nini. That was what all these apparently superfluous circumstances had to do with him and he owed them as much attention as was warranted by his relationship to her, his little pet. Or perhaps the awkwardness that arises when a person enters a completely new period of his life was behind this impression. If he overlooked the flaw on its west side—the empty, slanting, unutilized descent into the room—the walls themselves seemed all right to him, and that was at least something to justify the relatively high rent that she paid the fat landlady on condition that she not have any male visitors. Tjaž may have been a boarding school creature, but he was undeniably a male creature too. Only a proper boarding school student could have summoned enough courage to cast doubt on the beatitude and even the legality of women's rules and, at last, magnanimously ignore the fat landlady's resentful instructions. The second thing he experienced was that he immediately made himself at home between these walls. He acquired a fondness for all of the objects that stood, hung, leaned, or lay in the room, even though it was the first time he was setting eyes on them. When they walked in, their faces were accosted by air that the rays of the sun had been flogging all afternoon. Paying no heed to the impressions that her room ought to have richly showered on him at his first entrance, or to Nini's startled eyes which at that moment were expecting something entirely different, he tackled the window and amid much shaking of panes finally defeated its lock and threw it wide open. What rushed into the room wasn't the freshest or most soothing air, either, but it drove off the dense, battered stuff nevertheless, and billowed out pleasantly all over the furnishings. Nini threw herself into her household tasks, engaging in some fast-moving administrative procedures that completely absorbed her and would, he hoped, keep her away from him at least long enough for him to have a good look around this new place. Clearly too many images had forced their way into his field of vision at once, so much so that he couldn't deal with them all simultaneously, they startled him and he didn't know where to begin and how to start digesting them. He leaned on the window ledge, remaining present for the exchange of better air for worse that took place past his ears, and at last he focused on the window and all of the scenes that the window set out for his senses. The curtains fluttered from the curtain rod down onto his neck, where they divided into two streams. The fabric touched his skin generously and felt like two cold sabers with their blades grazing over his neck. This strengthened his conviction that they had hung at this window for generations and it acquainted him with disgust, because the same piece of fabric that was touching his neck now had touched others before— the necks of all the predecessors who had ever lived in this room. All the mornings and all the evenings they had reached for these curtains from the same place where he was doing that now. At first, in the full flower of their prime, they reached for them a little higher. But once age bent their backs, shortened their legs, and sucked dry their arms, they reached out for them lower and lower until, finally, they got so low that they couldn't reach the curtains at all. From then on they just drew them with their faltering eyes until, at last, they pulled them shut one final time. Like diligent bees they deposited the moisture of all the ages of their lives onto them. Even though Tjaž had seldom been this close to the source of life and though the lust for life had never poured out of him as powerfully as it did now, in the presence of these curtains he couldn't fend off reminders of transience. The building's roofs pressed their gray peaks right up under his window, and if he'd reached his hand out, he could have touched them. Smoke billowed bluish, gray, and red out of the chimneys, and high up above the slopes of the roofs swarms of mosquitoes and flies sharpened their stingers. Way down below the road sank away, late pedestrians with swift footsteps slicing it to ribbons. From up here it looked as though clumps of rowen, like the ones that spent the night next to the hedge in the meadow back home, were moving toward the barn. Dusk devoured the light and got fat on it, the sky sucked in the tips of the trees, and the trunks lifted their shiftless shoulders up into the young night. In an open area between houses bricklayers and cranes were constructing some big building. A crane lifted crossbeams, wall panels, and tubs of concrete way up over the pilings, a bulldozer stopped and a short while later the crane also lowered its iron hands, the cement fell silent, and the construction men's cars started coughing their way out of the worksite. Behind his back he noted Nini's sporadic movements, registering her rapid footsteps pumping away on their household rounds. They would move through the room first from one direction, then another, attacking it head on and from the rear, sneaking in a short pause here and there for the radio announcer to take advantage of, at times they would surface right behind him and then start a new furrow, which would retreat from his back into still undiscovered corners. He would guess at her movements without being able to get to the bottom of them, he would try to follow the migration of dishes but then lose track of them midway. He had no explanation for why she would want to prolong her time amid all these shoddy furnishings, he himself kept his business in the wardrobe, at the sink, and at table as brief as possible and carried it all out at only the most unproductive times of day. He would set one thing down, reach for another, move a third, and avoid a fourth, without once giving the impression that he gave them the least thought or had any particular love of neatness, such tasks didn't involve him, they stayed right on the surface so that he wasn't even conscious of them, while her they would take hold of insatiably, occupy her and drink the effort straight from her hands. It's true that he found his bearings amid these walls quickly, adapted quite a bit more than the bare minimum expected, developed a personal, almost homey relationship with them. It's also true that the attic room and all its animate and inanimate contents were predictable, they were extremely humdrum and banal, naïve beyond all expectation, not in the least exciting, and palpably distinct from the seductive, sophisticated, if involuntary image that his mind had created and his imagination had filled out. Yes, there were things in the world that fell beneath the standards of the boarding school and bore no relation to it. His idealistic, boarding school notions had been shattered, leaving less than remains of a soap bubble when it pops, and he had quite a few rungs down the ladder to fall in order to be standing on solid ground again. But he no longer dwelled on this fall from those honey-rimmed clouds, hoping instead that healthy forces would rescue him when the time came. He believed there were as yet untapped drives within himself that would transform him at just the right moment, and the fact that he was here in her room had to suffice as proof, he wished for those changes so ardently, and, what's more, he had resolved to entangle himself in this most mysterious net precisely on account of this ambition, he wanted danger and sought it out so doggedly that it couldn't resist him, he kept getting closer to it, and even when he could feel its breath on his cheeks, he went right on provoking it. The roofs that a short while before were shoving their dirty chimneys under his nose had retreated, revealing a view of a gigantic anthill, dotted with little bug lights and stretching out in all directions. These tiny points of light were now transforming countless workshops, elevators, cellars, bus stops, kitchens, golf courses, hallways, balconies, toilets, urinals, salesrooms, movie theaters, churches, printing presses, brothels, waiting rooms, warehouses, garages, cafes, hospitals, sacristies, slaughterhouses, entryways, auditoriums, stairways, shacks, rummage stalls, offices, bedrooms, graves, filling stations, attics, granaries—all was transformed by the dots of bug light into one vast swelling. His eyes reached beyond all this refuse of the magical night, into the distance, where they could wander homeless. The bonfire grounds of the darkness were throbbing, a spasm held back their flames, but they shook off the last reservations that stood in the way of complete liberation. Tjaž traced out his prey more distinctly, he spread out his belly and captured the sparks and held his breath as he waited for the warmth to slide down his skin, for his heart to be made fruitful with a full measure of love, for the bellows to stir up enough sparks for him to be able to get up from the window. This waiting was full of wicked pleasures, and every moment it ebbed and flowed. Because the end result of this waiting—just like the immediate future—was incomprehensible, and because one couldn't even guess at it, the tension was like nothing he'd ever experienced. At that moment the boarding school would have had to envy its ward Tjaž just as mightily as he then despised it. But no, he knew it was pointless to expect that kind of justice, his boarding school was never envious, because to envy was to admit your own weaknesses vis-à-vis some superior entity. All the same, Tjaž likewise had no cause to envy the boarding school, no, he'd just go on despising it. That night he bedded down so much more softly than others. At these moments his boarding school classmates would be fructifying their big, cold beds, they would disgorge the prescribed quantity of sleep into the chill air of the dormitory, they would dream of escapes from their wishes and worries, all while they belched their supper out of their stomachs. Whenever Tjaž was unable to fall asleep quickly and his fellow students' snoring beat him to it, he would be doomed to listen. The further night proceeded, the beastlier their snoring became. Such nights made him intimate with loathing and taught him to revel in it, he swallowed it down until he was overcome with drowsiness and, even as the vile music kept banging at his ears, he dropped off at last, under his blanket. Tonight they had probably already noticed the perfection of his untouched bed, had gathered at its foot, had gone to wake the director, and taken the steps that are called for in cases like these. They delivered him up for public discussion, his behavior was entrusted to the community for its critical assessment. It was clear that with this turn of events, his provision with all the comforts of the boarding school, those he had thus far enjoyed without restriction, must be called into question, his meals, his hot and cold running water, the laundering and ironing of his clothing, his reputation with the nuns, his use of the newspapers and magazines in the reading room, the space in the cellar for parking his bike, all of this was now at stake. He wore size forty shoes, always two sizes bigger than he needed, that's the size his well-meaning benefactors bought for him so he could get the maximum use out of them, but he never grew into them, let alone out of them. Henceforth he would have to buy his own. He risked whispers in his vicinity, discussions behind his back, and fingers pointing in his direction. The change that had unexpectedly turned the dormitory upside down had left everything open to debate, it even threatened the scratching abilities that were critical to his survival, of all possible blows the loss of his scratching gifts was the one he wouldn't recover from, if that source dried up, it would seal his utter defeat and his career would be over. It must have been some prize for him to cast all this aside and expose himself to such uncertainty, to leave this safe refuge and face the elements bareheaded, exchanging comfort for alarm, which, after all, could be triggered anytime anyway, as the result of some natural disaster—for instance, the attic room could collapse and bury both of them in its rubble, or he could be run over by a car. If, ultimately, the worst didn't happen, he might fall down some stairs and break a limb, nothing less serious than that could happen to him, for instance, if he got stabbed by the spear-like fence that zealously guarded the boarding school grounds and that he would have to climb over twice, first when he set out and then when he came back, he'd be stuck hanging there till morning when his schoolmates would discover him. Even before breakfast, then, he would have made their first good deed of the day possible, because they would take mercy on him and love him, though hating his sin, but he, blind brat that he was, wouldn't appreciate their kindness, just as he didn't appreciate all the other delicacies that had been leaping into his craw all these years, and he would laugh at the mercy being shown to him. They would drive the treachery and shamelessness out of him with the looks on their faces, they weren't going to rescue him off the fence quite so fast, they would jump back in disgust when the deed he had committed in the attic room and the dampness on his thighs gave him away to their generally refined sense of smell, which was particularly attuned to the scent of wetness from a woman's crotch. His very presence would threaten their boarding school virtues. But, ultimately, out of consideration for his peers and a learned sense of the importance of domestic tranquility, Tjaž relented and left them some hope that they had discovered in their ranks the biggest scandal of the past few decades. It's no longer certain where he first met Nini, whether while he was dreaming or while he was out killing his free time in the city parks, both are possible and each isn't so different from the other. He ran into her entirely by chance and, it goes without saying, this was entirely contrary to his convictions. There were rows of buildings encircling the park, and between them and the big piles of leaves streets darted and meandered through the autumnally tinted neighborhood. That day his eyes escaped through the park and set off at a sprint down one of the empty streets. Just at the point where they collided with the Sunday afternoon hollowness of the buildings, some barely audible footsteps behind him launched some leaves, which fluttered like feathers. Tjaž had not yet managed to summon his eyes back out of the streets when she had already passed him, sat down on an empty bench on the far side of the park, and crossed her legs, which shone like the legs of a bay filly all the way up to the bare thighs and down to the shoes. Despite his upbringing he decided to stick it out, more or less as an experiment, as in most such cases he willingly followed his instinct, the apple was hanging so close that all he needed to do was reach out and pick it, it promised an abundance of juiciness and it offered so many vitamins that it was becoming quite urgent that something be done for the sake of one's health. And so Tjaž held out to the end and put his boarding school virtues to the test, let them show what they're good for, and, what's more, this park, where he always sat on the same bench, practically demanded this sort of resolve. Perhaps somewhere else, in some other neighborhood, he wouldn't have noticed her arrival, but this park was his, he had appropriated it through countless sessions under its chestnut trees, so he always perceived visits by other people as a kind of breaking and entering. It was up to him who to exclude and who to share his property with. Two boys were making their way through the park collecting for the Red Cross. When they caught sight of him they approached and Tjaž uneasily parted with a few miserable groschen. After him the next and, as far as Tjaž could tell, the last of the boys' victims would be her. It struck Tjaž that the boys couldn't have found a nicer way to end their fundraising activity than with her donation. The can with the red cross on it relieved Tjaž as well as his prey of several coins, surely there was nothing unusual about that, but what was special was that here was an event that they were sharing, something was manifesting itself in both their lives for the first time and simultaneously, with the promise of long-term consequences. They were sitting across from each other. Any other day at this time he would already be back at school or at least on the way there, but today he stayed sitting, there was no place he had to go. Not only coins, but darkness too had accumulated in the can, the boys had gone, carrying off their collection but leaving the darkness for them, the first stars began dropping off the trees into the park, in all the buildings modest curtains were being drawn over the windows, the vehicles on the roadways turned on their lights, time was pushing them, something had to be done, but there's no more awkward and dreary person in the world than one who's in love. He was itching to draw attention to himself, but he couldn't stop the thumping in his chest which must be booming all the way to the far side of the park, and not only was this wobbliness strangling him, but he also realized that he wouldn't have the nerve to speak to her, his modest vocabulary, developed for entirely different purposes, couldn't withstand such a flood of feeling and so much anxiety. The available words, the ones they had them graze on at the boarding school, were completely useless for an encounter like this, Tjaž sent them to hell, to blazes with the boarding school and its vocabulary too. Instead of the most natural thing, in order to get to know each other better, they quietly, each to himself, pronounced their names and learned them by heart. Her name was Nini, a very easy, simple name, just *ni* times two, Nini. Then, after they exchanged names, a conversation developed that they conducted inaudibly, each from his or her seat, she from her side of the park and he from his, they carried it on without words, separately, each to each and across the entire length of the park, without exposing themselves to each other. I was counting on you to come, he said. I've changed, you haven't noticed, I know, it strikes you as strange when I say that, but you should have realized that I can't always come and that I won't, I'm not here at all, she said. Of course, I'd forgotten, completely forgotten, if I'd taken your living arrangements into account, I'd have figured out on my own that you wouldn't be here today, you simply couldn't tear yourself away, though when the leaves rustled I was sure you had come, but now I know you didn't, he said. You called me at the office, Nini, and you said, come today if you can, that's what you said, she said. It's true, that's what I said, I said you've got to come tonight, because it's Sunday and no one will be watching the park, it's been so long since we last saw each other, it would be best if you came late, but you've come earlier, no problem, you didn't want to keep me waiting, you went behind my back to that bench at the far end of the park and sat down, before that you rustled the leaves, rustled them so softly that I didn't know if it was you or not, and now you're here, the curtains are already being drawn in the buildings and the cars have turned on their lights, he said. I know, I saw the curtains being drawn, as though I were sitting in the park and waiting for the windows to be dark, she said. Those fellows just collected for the Red Cross, tonight of all nights, doesn't that strike you as odd, he said. Forget about that, why are you being evasive and changing the subject, you wanted to scent your skin with mine, that's all, isn't that true, tell me I'm wrong, it's such a particular scent, you said, she said. I still think that, do you recall we were always running out of breath, he said. Yes, it took my breath away, toward the end when both of us lost our breath you decided to go, you were in a big hurry, she said. What you describe is correct, but you do understand, I had my reasons, and then I really did go, it's what needed to be done, and you were smart to be so understanding, there was no need to quarrel, I went past the chestnut trees out to the street while you stayed here, and when I turned around and my fingers looked for you, like this, see, you were gone, you'd evaporated in the autumn fog, and soon after that it started to rain, he said. No, it snowed, she said. It snowed, I remember, it was the first snow, a warm, soft, happy snow, we couldn't sit on the benches anymore because it was snowing, your eyes turned dark and wrestled with the white snowflakes, he said. What's that supposed to mean, snow-flakes fall, it's what they do, they always fall, she said. They melted on us, each one, half on your face, half on mine, every snowflake, can you imagine that today, those generous snowflakes falling on both of us at the same time, as if a cake were being crumbled off some huge farmhouse table and every crumb rolled into both of our mouths, each one of them melting half in your mouth, half in mine, he said. Now I get it, that was what made you assume and quite il-logically that I might just come today after all, no, you were wrong, I really wasn't able to, she said. When the leaves rustled, I took that as a sign you were coming, he said. He was already walking Nini out of the park as the two benches shouted their loneliness into each other's plank faces, revealing their white teeth and grinning at each other from ear to ear, Tjaž could no longer see or hear this, he was accompanying Nini, and at the end of the road he said good-bye and repeated it several times, but there was nobody anywhere for him to repeat anything to or for him to see off. A dark, grainy thicket hovered over the buildings, and here and there some feeble light evaporating from the streetlamps below trickled up through it. Every now and then a late truck would lash at it from below with its tails of light. The lights retreated into their shells so that eyes couldn't reach them, instead colliding blindly with the mass of grit overhead. The walls of the city began to merge with each other, and roofs covered with shingles, tiles, or blocks, burdened down with TV an-tennas, flat and slanted, square-edged, rounded, elongated, and pointed, those with chimneys and those without started to run into each other, with weathervanes and lightning rods retracting their coxcombs, and driveways ramming into vestibules and hallways, in short, the buildings had trimmed their extremities. Tjaž could no longer tell where the park was hiding with its bench and chestnut trees, it was eclipsed down there somewhere amid short-lived oases of light that dispatched their dowries out through the darkness. Somewhere down there in the vicinity of the railroad crossing the atmosphere turned noticeably black where it filled with soot, and that's where the rumble of steel wheels came from, somewhere down there, off by itself, the boarding school had to be. After that, the fog got drawn down into the depression where Tjaž suspected the boarding school was. Tjaž couldn't make anything out anymore, it was apparent that the city closed by this time of day, the last people were putting on their pajamas, brushing their teeth, gargling and rinsing, smacking their peppermint lips, hanging their towels up, making a contribution at the toilet and flushing, turning on night-lights, commending themselves to their mattresses, and negotiating an agenda with their bedmate for the rest of the night. Tjaž released the curtains so that they collided with each other and bounced off his neck, his stalk was announcing itself and increasing the number of his digits, at the boarding school things were harder, they lay two abreast and sometimes they even had to resort to manual labor. As a result of this experience at the school Tjaž was well acquainted with the demands of his stalk, which struck him now as boundless. The pepper had struck and was beginning to take effect with twice the usual heat until it consolidated the tongues of its flame in his abdomen, it smoldered as though big wooden tubs of hot water were being emptied all over his body, as though the apertures of all his cells were gaping at a desert-hot sun, his skin crusts over and the crusts eat deeper and deeper into the healthy skin, while pepper drives out the pepper with pepper and fades away to a thin, peppery ache whose sore spots barely show traces of welts anymore. She didn't wake up when he left, his hands smelling of the dampness of her crotch, he didn't wash them, though he could have, but the sound of the water in the sink would have wakened her. She was sleeping her way down deep, through a whole series of floors and ceilings and carpets, through all the stories and cellars, through the dirt down into the roots of the trees and even deeper, she slept her way down to the iron ore, coal, and fire, offering her body with no pleasure to subterranean veins of silver, iron, and lead. He watched the sleep damming up behind her eyelids and wondered how many more units of sin could be thrashed out of him. This young, fleshy animal had shaken our boarding school student out of his stupor after he'd been cured through and through with valerian and incense. Even the kitchen helpers who worked in the dazzling presence of the nuns and then sat here and there on benches in the courtyard from two to five in the afternoon as they sunned their white flesh in the nuns' shadows—even they were no match for her. Beneath the half-rim of her eyelashes he could clearly see black crows circling under her eyelids, they were grazing across the sky, darting here, darting there, spreading their wings, thrashing the wind, diving straight down into the red sky, where they caught fire and then nose-dived, their feathers singed, straight back toward earth. He reached out both hands and when no burning crows collided with them, he became aware of his unspeakable solitude. He didn't know what to do with the dead crows that had flopped to his feet. He quickly picked them up and carried them out of the attic room and raced down the stairs. Out in the hallway he was startled by his own shadow mocking the falling crows and squawking treacherously to boot, it rolled under his feet, to be wound back up into the twilight of early morning. Doors opened in the stairwell, people stepped out onto the landings and from around corners footsteps commingled with the rattle of locks. Tjaž clutched the dead crows to himself, held his arms over their deaths, and slipped past the people. But the people knew everything, because people always do know everything, they were informed. Well look who it is, the crow killer, they greeted him. Outside in the street a new day had just sent up its first shoots, barely had it managed to turn on its light when early travelers were already grabbing it and stuffing it into their overcoats. The streetlights were still fastened to their poles, waiting to be replaced by the daylight, but out where the poles merged with the asphalt, there were still giant patches of night all around. He set out at a trot into the city streets. They weren't waking up at the boarding school yet, he pushed open the heavy, studded maple door and squeezed through the opening. Too late he remembered that he should have set the dead crows down by some wall or at some doorstep or in the hollow of some tree, in any case he should have got rid of them before coming back to the dorm, but now it was too late. He tried to walk noiselessly through the stone vestibule, and precisely at the moment when he thought he was making the least noise, he felt a hand on his shoulder and the crows in his arms screeched uncontrollably.

4.

A CHAPTER ABOUT
WOODSMEN

He set the crows down at the foot of a pillar under the choir loft, neatly arranging them so they didn't get in each other's way, and he fluffed up their black down, his fingers lingering on those feathers where death had already slept pits into their gloss as he explained to them in crow language how they would need to behave over the next few hours. Ever since they screeched, since returning from his sweetheart's to the boarding school, because somebody had put a hand on his shoulder, he became more cautious. Even though that hand didn't threaten his position in the school and, as it turned out, meant only the best for him, the crows really shouldn't have screeched quite so brazenly. It was extremely ill-advised, what they had done, and from that moment on Tjaž didn't let them out of his sight. He kept instructing them on what they should and shouldn't do and how to behave in this or that circumstance. The hand that came down on Tjaž's shoulder that evening was mine, in other words a thoroughly reliable, trustworthy, reasonable hand, though for him in the first split-second it was the unpleasant, hostile hand of a stranger. Tjaž didn't tolerate just anybody putting his paw on him, but in my case alone he overlooked this terrible rule. The story has progressed far enough for me to insert myself now without damaging the sequence of things, so it's time for me to introduce myself into these events. In the course of the years when the two of us were still under the same boarding school roof, we provided each other much mutual support and looked out for each other to help avoid the impact of any unforeseen incidents. He was the one who first introduced me to love, who gave me my first instruction in sexual matters, shared some expertise on intercourse with women, described his experiences and most of all enjoyed going on about the way you had to take hold of a woman and finish her, and how to fan her last little flames. I couldn't reciprocate except with occasional favors, because my father was a street sweeper and, as such, a public employee with a minimal salary, so there were no other advantages to him from knowing me, we were friends or at least accomplices, why, I don't really know, probably because of the very similar efforts we made to heap years onto the boarding school, that wizened, brick grandma who knew how to tell wonderful stories from the Bible and other, similar fairy tales, how to drive her wards out of the sun and into the shadows or from the shadows out into the sun, nurse them and cradle them and see to it that they didn't get dirty and poop in their pants too often, but that was the extent of her competencies. The boarding school was threatened, there was no doubt about that. While Tjaž pursued fleshly desires, as we technically referred to that business and learned to repeat in ever evolving contexts throughout the course of the year, while he pursued that very narrow domain, I pursued adventure in a much broader sense of the word. Tjaž came home from seeing his little pet, who had taken pity on his stalk, that maligned organ of the human body whose sole function is to pass water, while I at that time as a foe of all sports would go to the municipal field house to watch ice hockey, even though I felt as little connection to the sport as I did to all others, I would slap my knees with the best of them, shout myself hoarse, get chilblains on my feet, alternately inhale the game and the cold, think the whole time of my poverty, which didn't allow me any proper way of spending my time in the cold seasons, and the rest of the night I would warm myself in the company of drunken friends in some café. I got back home just before Tjaž, heard footsteps behind me, assumed they were our overseers', forced a hole in the wall and squeezed into it, held my breath, waited, spied, recognized, and breathed my hand onto the shoulder of a Tjaž who out of sheer caution was almost invisible, but then suddenly startled. Tjaž had developed indisputably more abilities than the others, as witness the traces he left in every field and, if need be, in the classroom and lecture hall too, where his fellow students, who were hardworking and exemplary, but otherwise dolts, liked to harass him. Yet in his domain Tjaž knew how to limit himself to the most basic human needs. His abilities, which included scratching and carnal intercourse with his little animal, were so focused that he didn't lag behind his peers, but rather they complemented each other splendidly. Where his fellow students had a diversity of pursuits and were thus forced to remain superficial, Tjaž in his monotony went much deeper, plumbed the depths, but the boarding school, deformed and menopausal, fortified against Greek fire, armed with boiling oil and gallows as it gathered in its army of crusaders, thwarted us all. That night Tjaž arranged the crows under the choir loft and instructed them in their assignment, then took a seat in the backmost pew and waited. A fishlike silence set in and serenaded our ears. The otherwise gray walls now appeared reddish and only in the places where they were covered with paintings and saints did the red transition into black. On the left, just to the side of the altar, hummed a lamp that was as red as communism, straining for all it was worth to feed the vast expanses, but in this it of course failed. At this hour the variegated windows were still off duty and merely twinkled at random. The pew that was burdened by Tjaž's rear end exuded a chill that did nothing to encourage the brain toward any particular activity, in the winter the church was pleasantly cool and in summer it was pleasantly warm, and in autumn or spring its walls exuded nothing other than pleasantness, which is a trait shared by every other church anywhere you go in our province. It managed to preserve roughly the same temperature year-round, a temperature that, while it kept the body vaguely awake, prevented intellectual zeal. No, the risk that the students might incur some inflammation of the brain was one that the boarding school didn't run, no students died of encephalitis. Tjaž surrendered to the ordinary, worm-eaten ideas that are the only viable kind under the choir loft at such a late hour. He was waiting for a shuffling through the side door to announce the arrival of someone. Though anyone could have walked in in that darkness, Tjaž didn't doubt that this was the right person, and the anxious sniffing of the crows confirmed for him that his assumption was correct. These footsteps were incapable of lifting off the floor, forsaking their soles, rebounding from their shoe leather as though it were the softest moss, no, they were incapable of that, but they did announce themselves firmly and often. They reminded Tjaž of his father, the way he shucked corn in a very similar way on autumn evenings. I realize I must have been walking very clumsily and carelessly, I understand if he thought it not at all out of the question that I might suddenly start slapping my thighs, in his eyes I'm sure there was nothing stealthy, nothing secret or mysterious in the way I walked, even though I did my very best to step carefully—instead, it must have been somewhere between the walk of a poet and that of a swineherd hauling slop with both hands. In any case, there was the mitigating circumstance of the terrible anxiousness that jolted through my arms and legs, though I knew that despite my nervousness I couldn't let myself get mired in fear. Tjaž would never have allowed himself to waste so much energy for nothing, any aimless flailing around filled him with disgust. At those moments, when first contact with the newcomer was being forged, he rued ever having harnessed me into the business. A little later we were standing opposite each other under the choir loft, each one trying to make out the dim shadow in front of him. Tjaž realized then that his regrets were only partly justified, because they derived from his own nervousness. Not that we could have seen into each other's faces, because we were gripped by a darkness as black as pitch, and we could only make each other out by the way each one breathed, perspired, and held himself, we each had an extraordinary ear for the other, the way we felt our way toward each other through perfect darkness without whispering a word. Tjaž's mouth stretched wide, which was a sign he was satisfied with me. It had been arranged that a good long time after Tjaž, at such and such an hour, I was to go through the back narrow door that led into the right nave of the church. We slept in different dormitories and for that reason had to agree in advance that we would leave separately. We had settled on the narrow door, because it struck us as safer and more appropriate. Otherwise, only eighth-graders had access to it, and all the other students had to pass through the side door or the main back door, but tonight that didn't matter to us, we had taken it upon ourselves to lower that boarding school standard. At that spot the wall was not only stupendously thick but the passageway could only be navigated in single file. Everyone who went that way had to shore up his confidence each day that this phlegmatic building was assured an enduring existence and the fattest possible typeface in the history books. It's understandable that the eighth-graders leaving the school for church were in greatest need of that reassurance. And it wasn't just the violation perpetrated by the narrow eighth-grader door, not just the wall of Babylonian proportions that took aim at the boarding school standards, but also the impression that it wasn't even a door you were walking through, but a rock fissure in some mountainside. For a while we sat unoccupied under the choir loft. What Tjaž had noticed a short time before, I noticed now, the exact same picture offered itself, the walls were still dark, the eternal light invitingly offered itself up to the saints and shone at their feet, even though they weren't going anywhere, Christ was spending the night on the high stump in the presbytery. Then behind us there was a knocking, someone was banging his fist on the main back door, Tjaž jumped to his feet, nobody had ever seen him open the door with such celerity, Nini came in from outside and with her a few streams of light trickled in under the choir loft without their tips getting stuck in the pores of the masonry. Tjaž put an arm around her waist and pulled, rather than simply let her inside, and in the place in the darkness where he suspected her cheek would be he planted a kiss, most of all because he thought that would make the biggest impression on me, what he cared about most was conveying explicitly enough what he had or lay claim to and pointing out all the attendant advantages to his deprived friend, he used his free hand to lock the door while the other arm curled around his little animal, and finally he pushed the long key down into his trousers. The crows caused no trouble, they'd been informed about her arrival, and we didn't lose any time, all three of us went down to the front through the ravine with pews to the right and left. Tjaž felt like he was walking down the aisle to get married. The uproar at the house of the bride's family was over, the heart-rending leave-taking was over, the watering can, the spinning wheel, the barber, the seamstresses, and the bride price were behind him, and all shame had been squelched, because now both houses had been able to sew their honor back up just in time, the wedding dress had been let out substantially, because the bride's belly was bulging out more and more each day, now she had a white wreath adorning her hair instead of those flowers that just prompted gossip, the child would have a father and be named for a saint, which one for the moment was still up in the air, it hadn't quite been decided which saint it would be, they would feed it Milupa, Dr. Reis, and powdered honey, they would try oat flakes, too, the diapers would have a decisive impact on the modernization of the household and maybe even lead to the acquisition of a washing machine. He imagined all the theatrics heading his way, now that he was the leading man. Whenever they showed themselves outdoors, she would have to shove her arm under his, that's what the rules prescribed from now on, she would feel the muscles between his elbow and shoulder, they would synchronize their gaits and step, together now, first with the right, then with the left, they would tense the same muscles, move the same bones, strain the same flesh, and veer in the same direction simultaneously, both of them always with the same force, the same speed, taking the same length of time, and they would share a last name, Nini and Tjaž So-and-So, how ridiculous it sounded, and their mail would be addressed to Mr. and Mrs. Such and Such, they would go to the market together, to the doctor, go jointly to mass, grow used to their pew, this pew has been in this family's possession for a hundred and twenty-one years, may it remain so for generations to come, what you own is yours, even if it's just a church pew, and mind that what you own stays yours, even if it is just a church pew, after mass they'll gossip in the churchyard or outside the rectory, three sentences this way, three sentences that, a smile to the right and a smile to the left, then a wave to the priest for good measure as he comes waddling out of the sacristy, then some coins for the ministrants as they waddle after the old hen, what matters is that the priest notices, he needs to know that you're generous and go to church, you've always given freely to support the church's needs, at last comes the final praise the lord and now let's go home, Mary's people have done their duty. These scenes terrified Tjaž, they made him embarrassed and ruined his mood. He brushed them all out of his field of vision, but the guests kept coming back for his wedding. The path from under the choir loft to the presbytery kept dragging on and the preoccupied bridegroom, who had inadvertently waded too far out into married life, now grumbled angrily about the wedding, the band, and the nuptial rites. Suddenly all thought of any wedding was gone, as the boys left the bride in the lurch in spite of herself and vanished into the sacristy, brought out a long ladder, set it up against the cross that towered up toward the ceiling from out of the concrete floor, and leaned it against Christ's ribcage. This ladder was part of the liturgical equipment and as such had been blessed for Pentecost. It gave the churchman access to the lower-level cobwebs, though of course it didn't reach to the ceiling or the most remote corners. The churchman would climb to its uppermost rungs and from there poke a long feather duster at the grime and the bug lairs. From this ladder the feather duster smote the dust and the vermin several times each year, because vermin reproduce quickly. Sometimes bats would cling to the shadowy ceiling and forget to leave in the morning, and then, when the young faithful arrived, start flapping their ugly cloaks. Because they drew the attention of those assembled, who should have been focusing all their senses on prayer, but instead, sitting beneath those suspiciously hanging little black casks, kept anxiously shoving and ducking their heads away from probable drop sites, the churchman was forced to use the long feather duster to reestablish equilibrium in the practice of the faith. At those times he would have to set the ladder up in several places and poke the feather duster around to force the bats to their feet. For Easter all the Christs had to be covered with purple drop cloths and for Pentecost linden switches had to be gathered, not for the curative tea that can be made from them, but on account of some weird whim of the liturgists, and this set the ladder back into motion, and after that preparations for Christmas began on its rungs. Tjaž never ceased being amazed by the fertile liturgical fathers who invested so much of their male hormones into these liturgical interventions, who kept revealing ever new symbols to the eyes of the faithful, linking these with heretofore unperformed gestures and poses—the imagination could spend itself in the liturgy unobstructed, generating nothing but a greater susceptibility to faith, and it fell to the liturgists to be forever providing newer and better incentives. Only when these didn't succeed would they warm and spice up the old ones, because they had to go with the times, if not ahead of them, church life must always be tastily prepared, wrapped in glossy paper and tied with a ribbon, so that what was in essence bitter and hard to digest would at least be outwardly appealing. This is where the linden switches acquitted themselves well. Usually new incentives were born and old ones were driven out on the rungs of that ladder, and since the two of us were fully aware of its significance, we handled it with the utmost care. It was very murky, and the interior of the church, as it seemed to us, had grown even darker as the night wore on. Tjaž began ascending the rungs, soon reaching the first row of saints and leaving them behind to alight on the next row a little higher up. Beginning at its midpoint the ladder started to bend and squeak rottenly against Christ's ribcage. Tjaž leaped from the ladder onto the altar and was suddenly perched among wooden saints who were reluctant to acknowledge his arrival, since they could tell it meant nothing good. If Tjaž hadn't stepped onto a creaky, badly nailed board, nothing would have moved at all, but as it was he forced the saint assigned to that board into a vertiginous bow, which was by no means intended for Tjaž, but was rather an attempt to regain its own balance—still, the nodding was a sign of goodwill and satisfied Tjaž. The altitude of the altar where Tjaž had appeared was a trifling mat-

ter for the saints and they had mastered it with barely a raised eye-
brow, but I suspect it put him in a bad mood, and their venerable
company gave him no cause to feel otherwise. Still, he gradually
recovered his composure, shrugged off the rough-hewn insolence of
his colleagues on the altar, reconciled himself to their ambition and
arrogance, overlooked their rudeness that verged on jealousy, and
for himself summoned a greater share of confidence and courage.
Soon he had made himself at home and was twitching his nostrils
to capture the sweet, soothing incense, inhaling it at full strength
for the very first time. The pews stood alone far below at his feet, he
couldn't make his companions out anymore and assumed they had
picked out a pew from which to watch him. All at once he wanted
to have a crowd that would come here burdened down with their
worries, lift their eyes up toward him, and begin to shower him with
unfulfillable pleas, and indeed some extraordinary things started
reaching his ears, assailing him and crowding around at his ears.
Because he wasn't used to this kind of work, it took all his effort to
distinguish one matter from the other and prevent any of them
from being lost in the crowd, my goodness, how this kept a saint's
life busy, how it tickled the nose and swarmed under the skin! Incense and valerian smelled downright revolting by comparison. Tjaž
lowered his eyes to the multitude, smiling benevolently and nodding solemnly, that was the least he owed them, then without further ado he took on their problems, arranging them neatly by
weight, magnanimously solving them as he sifted through them,
everyone got what was due to him, the multitude must have felt the
difference, since it was exposing itself in such numbers and devoting
so much of its herd instinct to this new, fresh breeze that cooled and
revived them. Tjaž opened his mouth, but he didn't need to say
anything, because the gospel lay on his tongue. Since the multitude's cast of mind was worldly and sinful and it was unable to boast
of much virtue in the conduct of its life, it could guess at the words
that lay ready in his mouth, it could pick them off the tip of his
tongue, so that all he had to do was open his mouth and every now
and then wave his arms joyfully. Don't put up with slavery, slights,

and humiliation, Tjaž's arms waved wildly, for every injunction demand a justification, satisfy yourselves whether it's necessary. Stand
up for yourselves whenever possible, don't pretend not to be home,
and don't deny yourselves the things your neighbor is enjoying, demand and insist, because nothing will ever just be given to you,
instead you'll have to wrest hold of it through the toil of your cal-
loused hands and hold onto it with the hard work of your brains. If
someone should strike you on the right cheek, shove him back twice
as hard in the ribs to repay the injustice. Don't touch sauerkraut or
rhubarb anymore, the only reason they stuff you with it is to keep
free thought, independence, desire, passion, and the desires of the
flesh from erupting in you, they cork up your instincts with cabbage
whose acids are supposed to corrode your stalks to the point that
they're useless, and they try to curdle your blood with milk so that
it stops circulating through your sodden veins and can no longer
produce the next generation. Say no to those afternoon field-trip
walks that spoil your Sundays and holidays, your free time, haven't
you already been on all of the nearby hill- and mountaintops and
peeked through the keyholes of every church in the vicinity? They've
fed you with masses and afternoon pieties and worn you out with
pilgrimages so that you collapse in your beds and are lost to every
normal thought, such as for instance the thought of that juicy young
girl you ran into by chance that time. This was probably the only
speech that ever came out of Tjaž. He had the impression that the
pews nodded thoughtfully and for a good while, his words had affected them so much. He felt the urge to invite them up the ladder
so he could show them there and then all the impotence of those
captured birds, some of which had iron rods driven into their backs
to attach them to pillars, they were helpless, they could do nothing
to lighten anyone's burden. Others stood on their own on gilt foot-
stools, it was one of these that Tjaž's careless behavior nearly knocked
into the depths, and if he hadn't had such a well developed sense of
balance, it surely would have happened. They would have stared in
amazement with him when they got their first view of the saints
from up here, as they skirted the flutterings of the light-winged little

angels, their eyes encompassing the copper-wire aureoles of the saints and alighting on their bald spots, which were covered with near-microscopic fly droppings. Once, when the prefect of a nearby boarding school performed mass here, Tjaž gave the man's back a good scratching. He ran through all the details. The man had just applied the last blessing onto the church pews and the hands of the people were hurrying to comply on their foreheads, under their chins and above them, the celebrant contentedly turned away from the congregation, thus exposing his broad back to all the church folk, and the women fixed their critical eyes, so knowledgeable about fabrics, on it and compared it to the stunted, bleary backs of their spouses, while the men were busy trying to negotiate a price for Majola, who was going to throw her first bastard calf this spring because she hadn't been able to avoid the bulls in the mountain pastures. Just as the church choir, after a brief scuffle with the organ, launched into the third verse of the hymn "Arise, Ye Toiling Youth," Tjaž aimed, from his place on the balcony, right at the back of this prefect's neck, planted his claws in his vestments, and pulled. With a squawk the fabric vented its outrage at the toiling youth, the haggling over Majola stalled, and the women all privately determined to try again with their husbands' backs. Tjaž gave another yank floorward and the man's linen outer shirt appeared, then his cotton undershirt, and then his skin, at which point Tjaž stopped, leaned out a bit over the choir loft to size up whether everything had been sufficiently peeled or if he should carry on and scratch the trousers off of those plump, well-fed lower end pieces, but then he decided against. Now, as he looks back on that event with more mature eyes and from above, he has to admit that he made the right decision. Just that much undressing had brought about such ringing cries, commotion, and quarreling, the director involuntarily exposing the farthest reaches of his mouth to full, unimpeded view, so Tjaž had to lean down just a tad more to be sure that they all had fillings. Christ had been stripped down to the bones without a complaint, not even a peep, while here there was all this raving over a few split liturgical rags. But this event had yet another alarming aspect,

namely that in the process of scratching Tjaž noticed to his amazement that his own body was growing, and growing with the same
passion that he applied to fulfilling his task, his bones began to pop,
his joints to shift, his tendons grew taut, his muscles lengthened,
and his skin burst into a sweat before giving way. There was no
doubt, Tjaž had begun to grow, to develop, to unlock his frame, he
felt a tension and tearing all through his body, the pain of it so exhausting him that he was useless for any other work the rest of that
day, his scholarly successes began to decline and his desire for food
multiplied. Whenever the gentlest breeze licked him with its cold
tongue, he had irrefutable proof that his body had grown again, that
its new parts had not yet adjusted to prevailing conditions and that
they needed to get acclimated. This unexpected discovery was decisive for the entirety of his remaining career, for at last there seemed
to be some chance that nature would make up for its delay and the
boy would grow into a normal person, because there was still time
enough for him to grow. What put the boy on uneasy terms with
himself was the marvel that he continued to grow only as long as he
kept up a particular bout of scratching, and the deeper he scratched,
the faster he grew, his growth being entirely dependent on the number and thoroughness of scratchings. There was even a danger of too
much growth all at once, propelling him from childlike retardation
to outsized gigantism, because his body wouldn't be able to keep up
with his own scratching and his twinges would overcome him. If he
wanted to prevent this, he had to limit his scratching to only the
most urgent cases. Even so, in those years he scratched most copi-
ously, he used his hooks countless times to feel his way over the
whole altar, in a very controlled way of course, he never let loose or
went wild, there wasn't a female saint who didn't get a hickey or
worse on her arms or her thighs, just as there wasn't a single male
saint who didn't have some memento of Tjaž. He scratched up An-
thony's piglet, Matthew's axe, Apollonia's tongs, Lucia's dish, Cath-
erine's wheel, Isidor's flail, Juliana's alder branches, Magdalena's
whip, and Hieronymus's Slovene-German dictionary. Most of all he
liked to spend time with the female saints, among whom the virgin

saints made out best of all, and there were plenty of these in the boarding school's chapel, they were arranged according to the weight of their virginity from the front to the back, with those who were entirely virgins occupying the foremost places of honor, while those who were almost virgins had been pushed by the liturgists—quite undeservedly, it would seem—into the corners. But even there Tjaž's scratching claws found them out and relieved them of a few saintly appurtenances. The classmate who lost his shoes that time had been the target of the first scratches, but after that Tjaž had scratched a lot at assemblies, lectures, gatherings, campouts, fairs, meetings, elections, on pilgrimages and field trips, he had scratched in simple rooms and in big, bright auditoriums, in overstuffed stores and in sparsely supplied way stations, in manor houses and on farms, in cabins, shacks, and palaces, in the street, in workrooms and offices, in public and private places, sometimes scratching more, sometimes less, just as much as he wanted and as much as seemed necessary for his physical growth. At first he lacked discernment and he often scratched too much or even unnecessarily, on a number of occasions scratching straight out of the blue. Over time he adapted, and it became rare for him after serving his daily eighth penalty hour to feel that he'd exceeded his quota. Time made no difference to him, he scratched by day and by night, best of all in the evening, and he scratched both summer and winter. He performed many of his scratchings in passing and doesn't recall them today, they've passed into oblivion, but many others remain imprinted on his memory. Particularly vivid is his recollection of the scratching at the printing press. He had been sent there to pick up some printed material for the boarding school and at first Tjaž had no inkling that those huge rollers stinking of oil and ink could inspire his scratching nails, and anyway he had just racked up a full week's worth of scratches. The whole mechanical installation shook when the powerful Swedish rollers turned, the barely audible electric motors hummed steadily, a suction device fed white sheets of paper into the teeth of the insatiable rollers, pneumatic equipment stepped in where necessary, and the hands on the clocks hurtled along, dipping their tips into various fields of color. The moving parts rose up and reached out, inducted and emitted, squeezed and stretched, slammed and puffed, tautened and clanged, performing first in chorus, then solo, until they finally stretched out their steel limbs and breathed their last, not because they'd been worked to death, but because it was time for the employees' break. When Tjaž arrived, they had just finished printing a color poster. The director, whom Tjaž hadn't found in the office, and the printers were standing around it, unable to sate their eyes on the abundance of colorful beauty covering every inch of the paper. Given this printing sensation nobody had noticed Tjaž's arrival, and the newcomer had the sense of being present at the birth of an unprecedented technical miracle that was about to set out from this happy press into the wide world and conquer it overnight. He pushed his way toward the printed sheet but got stuck in the crowd and was unable to get close to the object of interest, unable to move forward or back, and suddenly the thought of scratching occurred to him, but because of his cramped circumstances he had to let it go for the time being. With his former, underdeveloped body he would have been unable to push even a step ahead in this instance and he would have bounced off the wall like a ball, but he had his fingernails to thank for the fact that he had grown some lately and that he could at least visually size up his immediate surroundings—even so, some of the printer's apprentices still outmeasured him by half a head or more. As much as he tried, he wasn't up to the poster, he couldn't elbow his way close enough to make anything out, he was dependent on what the others were saying, and there was more of that than he thought necessary to determine the poster's message, and in this respect he was hearing everything: either it was inviting the public to an auction of Pinzgauers or it was announcing a white sale and discounts on summer shoes, who knows, some people even thought the poster was for an important congress of the National Union, a very enthusiastic party for the people, advocating the support and suppression of political and cultural rebirth. The printer's proofreader, who in his free time sat on committees of a society of Catholic-oriented mountaineers, dreamed of a poster like, or almost like this one to announce the upcoming meeting of the society's executive committee, and at the thought that he might be elected on the occasion to a higher office, he was overcome with stage fright. The text of the poster might just as well have been summoning everyone to some sweet little cultural event, whether a nice little play or a nice little concert, or it might have been advertising some new brand of rat poison. But even some new-fangled spinach seeds, the war against nettles, promises of cosmetic perfection and artificial manures were not out of the question here—who knows, in fact, what the printing press had just finished printing that it was able to touch all those present so much and yet about which they weren't able to agree. At the point when the opinions started contradicting each other the most, some nuns came scurrying out from the editorial offices to dip their wings in this colorful business. Nuns always made Tjaž's fingers itch and it took all his available strength to restrain them so they didn't go wild, whenever a nun interrupted his daily routine the urge to peck began announcing itself and this time was no different, he distinctly felt his nails starting to twitch. It was the good sister editors and proof-readers themselves who saw to it that he could oblige those nails so soon and give them a green light, the people must see this, these are the colors that will help us get our message across. To this day it remains unknown if the sensitive poster in question found its way to the people despite the incident that followed, in any case the boarding school students looked for it all vacation long and still couldn't find it pasted to any storefronts, and what's more the actual content of the poster remains a mystery to this day. What has been established for certain is that Tjaž hadn't been recruited to undertake this act of sabotage, but was carrying out a mission of his own. He picked out the newest Swedish machine that had taken Swedish engineers three whole weeks to install, and he removed all its levers, handles, rungs, shelves, and rollers, scratched out its screws large and small, its nuts, bolts, cogs, wheels, panels, and covers, they all simply collapsed, the machine wheezed and coughed and clattered terribly, as first the motor's protective housing went flying apart, then a belt shot like a bullet toward a box of paper, and then massive heaps of iron, steel, tin, wood, and plastic liberated themselves. Even before the printers jumped back and the good sister editors hiked their mantles up out of the way, a mixture of colored inks and oil spilled all over the colorful poster. For the most part the scratchings were spontaneous at this time. All sorts of things would come up to attract Tjaž's ill will and embolden his nails, and he did a lot of planning so that his scratching followed a well-defined sequence. The obliteration of neck chains must be counted among his regular tasks. The boarding school's students faithfully hung them around their necks, but Tjaž couldn't stand this and was ruthless about them, secular symbols such as horseshoes, four-leafed clovers, chimney sweeps, and mushrooms he found just as revolting as saints, the only exception he made was Christ, whom he'd leave dangling in his scant linens. Evenings, when the boarding school washed, exposing a maximum of skin, Tjaž would make a quick circuit of the sinks to memorize all the amulets around necks. The instant an opportunity came the following day, he would plane the chains off those necks and send them pitching down through shirtfronts, under belts and out through trouser legs. Sometimes his fellow students didn't even notice and only felt that their neck chain was missing, most often later that day they would discover some meager remains, a few links of the chain that had caught in the folds of their underwear on the way down. Tjaž no longer used the ladder, but made his way up the altar by climbing from one of its platforms to the next. When he felt that the altar's structure could no longer support him, he stopped and dunked his head into a cumulus in the first row of clouds that gathered around, building up toward a rainstorm. Tjaž spread his legs slightly apart, which meant he was getting ready to go on with his work. He set the saw down right over his head and shoved it into a cloud that already belonged to the icy realm of the cirrus, but its teeth bounced off before they could bite a path into the wood, and some sawdust suddenly blew in Tjaž's face, got caught in his sleeve and shirt, and sprinkled into the depths. It drizzled past the nimbi and aureoles that the saints had borrowed from their Greek colleagues of pagan origin but have still, to this day, forgotten to return. In the meantime the saw took hold of the wood and dug into it, sneezing groats out through its teeth. Soon, down below, near the floor, another saw started to sing in the area assigned to me. While Tjaž took care of the higher saints, I sawed away at the lower ones. Both of our implements ate into their targets as the song of the woodsman's tools filled the room. We lashed our saws through the wooden bodies with such zeal that no second thoughts could take root in us and obstruct our logging, without sparing a single one we mutilated the bodies that were reachable by saw, sawing numerous limbs in two and sending the saints' wooden extremities flying to the floor, where they crashed onto the flagstones and carpets, flew apart, and bounced through the church as far as the pews or smashed into a wall, while up in the altar the maimed remnants of bodies resembled trimmed and topped tree trunks jutting in all directions. When, as if on command, five or six searchlights suddenly shone on us from every doorway into the church, our work was mostly finished, and while a few of god's saints still waited, offering us their wood, we weren't able to zing through it anymore, because the searchlights had beat us to them. Tjaž removed his saw without sawing through what he had begun, and I was also caught hanging on the ladder's lower rungs, and a tomblike silence ensued amid which only the breathing of the two woodsmen could be heard and the abrupt pauses in our breath. The police searchlights guarding the exits shone noiselessly, the silence stiffened, the corpselike colors hardened, eerie creatures waved their arms from the pews, and whenever the beams of light intersected, they pierced only the darkness, but not the silence. As they frisked our faces, the poisonous light stinging our eyes, we felt like lunging at it and strangling it. But our feet didn't move. A woodsman's silence responded to the tomblike silence. The saws had stopped echoing, the wood had relaxed. Even the voice that erupted to order our nighttime gang not to move didn't disturb the torpid air, its mouth opened commandingly wide and the words spun around inside without a single one breaking off and escaping.

At the very least the crows beneath the choir loft could have easily squawked at the top of their caws, but they were bound by Tjaž's instructions. In the swaths of the powerful searchlights as they darted back and forth among the sawed-off saints' limbs strewn all over the floor or glanced over the stumps and trunks up under the ceiling, we couldn't distinguish objects from emptiness.

5.

A CHAPTER ABOUT
THE LAST SCRATCHING

He had imagined his departure from the boarding school would be a lot simpler than it in fact was. This report about Tjaž would be shorter and limited to only the most notable events were it not for the fact that even superficially extraneous matters turned out to be notable and essential. Consequently it is impossible to pass over them, and precisely they will weigh down this report and make it longer. You see, to make things short we could say that the time Tjaž spent living at the boarding school was coming to an end, and our business would be done, the report would be concise, factual, interesting. But in fact the time Tjaž spent under the boarding school roof was not coming to an end, it wasn't even making any effort to come to an end. Or how would one put it: racing to its end? It's entirely possible that the individual who commissioned this report would strike through phrases like that, or maybe even reject the whole report on account of them, and perhaps dismiss me and go find some other, more dependable report writer. I realize that the report has to be reliable, factual, and well executed. If I lose my daily bread, I'll choose some other profession, and it wouldn't have to be a profession at all—any white-collar or even blue-collar job would do. I've been thinking about becoming a truck driver, or selling vending machines, or hawking subscriptions to some book-of-the-month club. At least there I could avoid the mistakes and pitfalls that I'm exposed to here without my knowledge. His time was coming to an end really doesn't mean anything at all, and if we were to insist on turns of phrase like that, it would serve me right if the boss fired me. I have to keep the standards and wishes of my superior in mind, and in this case that shouldn't be hard at all, why, I myself see that a phrase as simple as that doesn't sit right, doesn't do justice to the actual state of things, doesn't serve up the right image. A birch rod, a bottle, a pencil, a telephone pole can all race to an end, but it would be questionable to make the same claim for a stream, a flower, or a hallway. A pencil can be racing to its end, sure, you can force it to do that, but you'll have no such luck with a hallway, it won't accept that, these things just aren't as simple as we might like them to be. The problems leaving the boarding school began with his ass, even though the boss might not believe it, but that's how it was, on account of his ass Tjaž's time refused to enter its twilight phase and wasn't even preparing to do so, it just floated on the surface like fat floats on soup or pre-Lenten doughnuts in grease, there was no getting it out of its rut. It saturated the wood of the pews and the chairs, the fibers of the floorboards, the crevices between the tiles and logs, it varnished every object that the nuns wiped the dust from as a result of their perpetual vows, the dust of course responding in kind with its own perpetual vow. The report is closing in on some key conclusions: because everything that the skin secretes when it sweats was absorbed in the wood, it could not be erased or taken along with you, even though it was personal property. There was a link between these two facts—between the skin's generosity and the wood's absorptive powers—just as there is between cause and effect. The one conditioned the other. Because the skin secreted sweat, the wood absorbed it and vice versa, because the wood absorbed sweat, the skin secreted it. A person isn't just an asshole, not just fat, but also blood, bones, and body. Perhaps it's escaped you thus far that everything a person is, aside of course from what he isn't just, begins with *B*, yes it has, hasn't it, as attentive and detailed-oriented as you may be. A person would be far more integrated if all the other parts of his body began with *B*, but they refuse, they have reservations, and it's fine that they have reservations and refuse to begin with *B*, because to do so would be truly stupid and alphabetical violence, and we're against that, what are we against, we're against alphabetical violence and we'll see, perhaps we already have, let's vote, down with violence, down with it, by force if necessary. With the bones it's different, bones don't leave traces in church pews or classrooms or lecture hall benches, but they do leave traces on the human body, and that's violence too, I propose violence, let's vote on it, because they drill pits into elbows and knees, they mark the body, and vice versa, because their task is to mark it, they drill pits into its elbows and knees, and here I must remind the boss of a word that denotes a body part in which *B* figures prominently, el-bow, he's grateful to me for just such insignificant footnotes and marginal glosses. While the pits are of no value, being general and non-distinct, we mustn't underestimate the value of holes. There are people who are ashamed of the hole in their ass and resent it, most likely because they have no understanding of it, because they're ill informed about it, because they aren't up to date. This hole is not just part of an organ ensuring our health, not just the exit point for everything that has been introduced to the body, it's also one of the few passages that would seem to be one-way only, and as such it stands as an irrefutable proof of the fact that the wood isn't just hard, but also soft and thirsty as a dry sponge, because otherwise how could it suck in all that moisture from the skin. There is no alternative but to shove all the boarding school boards aside, such as they are, fed and watered and swollen from sitting, and fart on them one last time. A fart like that softens the smell of the incense, the holy water, the brass candlesticks, and the moth-eaten fabrics, a fart like that neutralizes the air a bit, disinfects it and cures it, making it breathable. So it'll be no problem for him to shake off the dank walls, concrete floors, and ceilings covered with paintings. No, he won't be able to take anything away from this place anyway but some disinfected air, pits and holes, some smoke and scents that his clothes had absorbed and that had collected on the inner walls of his nostrils. And one good nose blow will take care of that. Cici had a hole up front between her legs which, if anything, more resembled a slit or a cleft, and why shouldn't it, but in the end it was a hole. At that age Tjaž could already distinguish a pit from a hole and he knew what the one needed as opposed to the other. Whenever Cici cleared the tables and carted food out of the elevator, whenever she swept the hallways or went to fetch some forgotten thing that she hadn't forgotten, the boarding school students understood why they had a bit more flesh in the same place where Cici had a little less. She was on intimate terms with the kitchenware, she had a pimply face and pimply limbs, she wasn't comely of face or of body, but that didn't matter, on the contrary, so much the better to fulfill the terms of her appointment in the establishment. Only the hole couldn't be removed, like it or not they had to let it in with the rest of her, because aside from that fact she'd do fine. They could also have hired a man and avoided the hole that way, but that would have increased the expense and involved a whole array of other complications, so an eyesore like Cici proved cheaper on all counts. If Cici hadn't been hired, the boarding school boys would most certainly have imagined the hole differently, but because Cici was hired, they imagined the hole as they did. She had so much to do with the dishes, the elevator, and the forgotten things that she hadn't forgotten that she didn't understand the boarding school boys from the start. Good evening, off to bed with you, good night, I'll be off now. They took to informing and teaching her, and to those lessons they added bits of advice and learning aids. Good evening, off to bed with you, good evening, I'll be right there. The boarding school students redoubled, hardened, and squeezed the lesson, and now Cici understood and provided them with some new experience, decidedly influencing their notions about the hole. Tjaž had no cause to make a lot of fuss over taking his leave. He hadn't grown attached to this place, so he wouldn't have to tear himself away from it. He would clean up after himself, for sure, but no more, if a person does a thorough job of cleaning up, that's leave-taking enough, buckets, brushes, and brooms are signs enough of farewell. These tasks, the use of these objects unavoidably forces him into the poses and gestures that belong in the domain of leave-taking. His hands smooth the walls, the floor, and the furniture, they feel every single little crack and crevice through the dust rag, they never registered them before, but now the walls are full of cracks, now the floor is full of crevices. In the walls' indentations they rummage around in spite of themselves for little pockets of warmth, closeness, and comfort, though these things never piqued their interest before. How little pockets of warmth, closeness, and comfort could be of use to anyone at the hour of leave-taking is beyond me, they probably aren't, it's probably too late for them to be of use, I'll ask the boss for his opinion, he's the one who foisted this report on me and he has certain expectations of it, so let him decide what is and isn't important. I did ask the boss his opinion and he's against it—what does that mean, he's against it. It doesn't strike him as significant, and it's his right to decide what's important and what isn't, that's why he's the boss. No, I didn't ask him anything, why should I, I didn't ask him for any sort of advice, let alone a decision. Why should I go asking him for advice and forcing him to make decisions, how pointless is that, what could I expect of his answers, nothing. He's entrusted me with this task of providing him with a report about Tjaž, and how I do it is my business. How you do it is your business, he told me, word of honor. I'll get it done, I'll produce a report about Tjaž, about the various forms of Tjaž, about the number and tenses of Tjaž, about his modes, types, variants, and everything that is Tjaž. And with that the matter will be settled and the jurisdiction determined. Of course he could also rush me and set deadlines and standards, though that would drive up the cost of the report, which again would be his business, but I'm not working for free. I'd like somebody to show me a single other occasion upon which reliable facts have been gathered in less pleasant circumstances and with this much haste. He'll understand. I haven't asked him a thing. When I've finished, I'll send or deliver the report to him, I don't yet know which, he'll rely on it, he'll be informed, and he'll get an overview of the whole affair, he'll have to rely on it, on my facts, and not me on his. He's fully aware of this, so he won't let me ask him about anything, instead he has questions for me, how do I see this or that, what strikes me as important or not important, what standards have I used to assess and select, and whether I was able to reconcile those things, put them in context, contextualize them, contextualize them. I told him that I'm not yet a hundred percent sure. He's easy to work with, he'll give me a hand without sitting on me, he lets me work, and he doesn't get in the way and interrupt. At the boarding school they were always sitting on you at the same time as they were giving you a hand, that's the difference. Good morning, Cici, how did you sleep, if only she'd said wonderfully, sweetly, heavenly, every young girl sleeps wonderfully, sweetly, heavenly while she's still a young girl, but Cici and the boarding school students got their language mixed up and that was the end of a good night's sleep. Although they weren't conversant with even the most basic tools of the mason's trade, such as trowel, plumb-line, mortar, and brick, the boarding school still mixed up their language. So he's not about to go licking its thresholds, he's not going to hunch over in sorrow and snivel over the doormats. As he walks across the room with his bucket, brush, broom, and dustpan, his footsteps resound hollowly, they echo emptily, they lack substance, he gets in their way, he squelches their whole sound, it's time for him to get out of here. His face juts forth from his head, his neck sticks out of his collar, his back hunches, and his heels grow out into space, his hands tremble as he scrubs the floor kneeling, all these are sufficiently powerful if empty signs of farewell, all these are phenomena that aren't associated at all with free will, so this kind of behavior right before his departure from the boarding school is pardonable. What Tjaž did during his last hours at the institution was more like getting unharnessed than leave-taking. After all, we don't say that a horse takes its leave when it kicks over its traces, bursts free of its bands, gnaws through its reins, shakes off its backstrap, crupper, and belts, when it throws off its horse collar and splits the shaft into two or five, such simple calculations as dividing a shaft by two or five a horse can do in its sleep. Tjaž came unhitched the way a horse comes unhitched when it settles accounts with its master. He did it quickly, without any ado, diversions, or concealment. Free and unburdened he steps through the doorway, his shoes barely touching the threshold, his suitcase sensible, indulgent, not dragging on the floor. All his belongings have been stuffed under one lid, thank god the suitcase consented to that, he's not, after all, a pilgrim or traveler, he's a student who at this moment is expelled from the boarding school, a captain in retreat, a refugee, explosives, a bomb, all these things in one and all at once, he doesn't endure, he just occurred once and for all other times, this happened to him—no, that's wrong—he happened to himself. One suitcase is more than enough, what would he do with more luggage, why should he have to wear himself out dragging it through the streets of the city? He goes down the steps in a misshapen suit that bulges around him, in those curled-up shoes that have lost any connection to their owner, without any boarding school badges or diocesan medals adorning his jacket. Outside the autumn colors will latch onto him, or perhaps icy dragons will whisk him along on their powerful paws, maybe it's spring outside or summer or maybe not one or the other, maybe nothing at all, his exclusion from the boarding school doesn't align with any season, any month, any work or holiday period, the calendar has met its maker, gone barren and turned up its toes. Tjaž will enter a temporal void, a space of timelessness, time is fed up with him, fed up to here, has had it with him. His expulsion before the end of the school year had nothing to do with time, but instead with the way, the manner in which the boarding school expelled its wards—the answer: before the end of the school year. The boss claims that the time when they threw Tjaž out of the boarding school has no significance, that's what he claims, but that's awkward for me. I know the boss says that to make himself feel better, he doesn't mean to rebuff me, because this report means a lot to him, even if it will be deficient. I feel bad because I'm not making progress with the report, the issue of time doesn't bother me, I know that point can't be resolved, because there's no way I can approach it, the whole thing is stuck and is going to drag on into the unforeseeable future. All this unpleasantness could have been avoided if the institution had only understood Tjaž's warning and taken it into account. Tjaž wouldn't have incurred this disgrace, and the report itself would have been a lot shorter, and consequently that much more interesting, concise, and to the point than it's going to be now, because it's going to get bogged down in details. We have to grant him that he alerted the house to himself in plenty of time, that he distanced himself from it and warned it, but they refused to believe him, they believed in him staunchly and kept trying to win him over, now more deliberately than before, they didn't retreat from him, they had overblown expectations of him, instead of just hocking him out into a spittoon or spitting him out in a wide arc onto the trash heap. He had hinted in that direction numerous times, but they understood his later admonishments no better than the first. It's not what they wanted, and only now do they see it and realize that his first declaration was the clearest of all, he delivered it one morning as the ceremony in the boarding school chapel was moving along just fast enough to keep from grinding to a halt. Penitence was just over, though a few here and there were still repenting, even though they had nothing to repent and were mainly repenting for not having anything to repent. A few here and there were renouncing the evil they'd done and that they had to have done, because otherwise they wouldn't have been able to renounce it. Noses jutted up from the faces as incense dawdled across the ceiling's coffers, stretching out into various zoological shapes. Whenever there was a waft of an especially big chunk of incense or a particularly ample blob of wax, the boarding school students' noses all wrinkled a bit, at that moment resembling the muzzles of young oxen that have just picked up the scent of a plump young heifer. I'm not thinking here of Cici and her colleagues of the same ilk, not at all, Cici had since changed pastures and bulls and moved on to other uplands. Minute granules of sunlight sifted through the gaps in the curtains, I can't recall if it was a spring or winter sun that poured past the curtains. No, those curtains are out of place, they're not allowed here, what presumption, hanging curtains in a church, draping church windows, impossible, cross that out right now, instead let's say: minute granules of sunlight, whether springtime or winter makes no difference, sifted through the elongated, screened, and I believe also stained glass windows, they grated precipitously down the walls of the church, raising a considerable racket. Regarding the stained-glass windows I would reluctantly add that they must have been a very cheap grade of stained glass, probably a stainless stained glass, because I don't remember them anymore. It raised such a racket that the noses of the young oxen jumped off their faces, running this way, running that way, establishing contact with their neighbors and with the neighbors of their neighbors' contacts, while the yellow light dripped onto them—no—hurled its splinters onto them from the ceiling and walls. Attendant circumstances suggested that the spiritual address was about to begin, what a spiritual address is I don't know, and how should I know, I have no idea, I do have some vague notion, an impression of what it is, but I don't know. It's probably something highly poetic, its name would justify that assumption, that should do, *nihil obstat*, let us continue. Bones started to pop and the woodwork to creak as bodies sat up all through the church. After that the whole church stood up and stayed silent. But before the voice spoke, before the first little lyrical word was pronounced, it happened. It was as though the whole church was shaken at once by a mighty jolt, which the adults identified as a natural catastrophe, like floods or arson, and the young folk associated with a nasty, deep-reaching dentist's drill. The upstanding youth turned around in a trice and their faces alighted on a sleeping and snoring Tjaž. His hands propped his skull up so that it wouldn't roll into the breviaries of his neighbors to the right and left. Tjaž slept the sleep of the just, which is a sign of health and youth, he had never been seriously ill, his father's strap had tempered his physical health. The boarding school students had no time to form a proper picture of how something like this could have happened, and only later, after the dentist's drill resurfaced from the depths of the tooth, came to some modest, timid conclusions—no, they were incapable of bad, damaging conclusions, they were incapable of malice, but they were practical people. The very first instant after the dentist's drill bade adieu to the roots down at the base of the jaw, they could see that Tjaž might be useful to them if they could figure out how to position him right and make proper use of him—not the Tjaž who was their peer, but the Tjaž who had shown up at morning mass with a hangover. Outwardly, of course, they would have to condemn his carousing and the show he made of it this morning, that part was easy. They shared books with him, hallways, light, and air, and on Sundays they went with him on walks, they sat in the dining room, slept in the dormitory, stood next to him in the lecture hall, so there were plenty of opportunities, the maids did his laundry and linens for next to nothing, they would sew on his buttons for free, everyone had the highest opinion of him without expecting any payment in return. He was incapable of responding in kind, he didn't know how to adhere to the golden mean, to keep within bounds, all this was beyond him. Until then they had put up with him, taxed him only with brotherly kindness, showered him with understanding. He started to threaten the home, and all he accomplished was that the home started threatening him, he was going to have to perish in this unequal fight, that much he could have added up on his fingers, they would do away with him, extinguish his name just as abruptly as it had ignited years before, they would tame this little tempest splashing around in the sewer. First the institution would have to take measures, since it had been officially attacked and affected, then the boarding school students themselves would take measures, each in his own way, a few pithy gutter phrases would suffice for them to distance themselves openly enough. Internally Tjaž's indifference promised to benefit them greatly, they expected a rich harvest, this was a unique and flattering opportunity. But what am I saying, indifference, this wasn't indifference anymore, this was deliberate, brazen rebellion, malicious parasitism, still worse, provocation. The more they escalated in their condemnation of his infraction, the more they grew and gained worth in their own eyes, the rottenness of the former pleasantly soothing the rank greed in the blood of the latter. There was no doubt that with such a juicy shank the lion's share would fall to them, they would advance two or three rungs on the ladder and for the average boarding school student that's no mean feat. It was in the nature of an incident like this that they would compare themselves with Tjaž, examine him from all sides and sift through his various aspects. The profit from those comparisons would not exactly flatter Tjaž, it would be devastating for him while profitable for them. All their forced anger subsided and they stopped wishing him punishment and unpleasantness, they needed him to be as he was, because only that way would he be useful, they needed him sleeping and cold so that his cold breath would jolt them from head to toe, the way fever shakes a sick person, they needed an unbeliever who had sawed saints' heads off and written instructions for Christs, they needed a proletarian who had logged through their church, scratched it with his claws and his logging equipment, marked it for demolition and its statues for removal, they needed a handyman who had buried his nails in shoes, printing presses, liturgical vestments, shoulders, backs, and necks, they needed someone unchaste, who had given his twenty-first digit plenty of exercise instead of lashing his senses into submission. It isn't hard to picture how fat the other students got, just looking at Tjaž asleep. Then the long-awaited address began, overstrained with confessional asthma and phlegm. This sort of speech no longer got at Tjaž, he was free and well rested, and he no longer felt any burden, he was light, so light that at any moment he could have taken flight like a skinny balloon. At last he stood outside the door. Whether it was morning or evening, whether the sky was clear or overcast, whether it was a sad or a happy day, whether the leaves of the chestnut trees scattered a little shade on the street, I have to reply that I don't know for sure. Whether Tjaž set down his suitcase and nylon bag, in which the dead crows were trying to find as comfortable a position as possible, whether he set down his luggage next to the door of the ice cream parlor, preparing himself to receive his vanilla and raspberry ice cream with both hands, the ice cream attendant doesn't remember, she claims that a skinny boy stepped shyly into the ice cream parlor carrying such and such luggage, set it down next to the door and asked for ice cream. What does it hurt for us to believe the ice cream attendant. I make no mistake—I know this for sure—when I say that he got vanilla and raspberry ice cream, that he held it with both hands and that this was the first thing he bought as a free man. Nothing is known about what else he may have bought. After this visit to the ice cream parlor he manages for a time to erase every trace of himself, at least partially. He headed down the first road that goes past the institution, that's what I think. Every road leads somewhere—if not to the center of town, then to its outskirts. That's how it's built, so it leads somewhere, every road either takes you away or brings you somewhere, or both, which is to say that it takes people and objects away from each other, and then it brings you to another road, where it starts all over. Tjaž didn't care where the road led, from whom it was going to separate him and to whom it was going to bring him, the main thing was that it led him away from here, as far away from this place as possible. That's why it didn't matter which road he took and what side of the road he walked on. What was important was that he walked, that he let his legs have their fun, got them excited with some new rhythm or direction, varied their amplitude. Hello, how's it going, god bless, on we go. He turned this way and that, shifted the suitcase from his right to left hand, at the same time as he shifted the nylon bag with the dead crows from his left to right hand, so that the suitcase and bag met at his navel. He used church towers to get his bearings, but then he gave up that method and decided that from now on he would get his bearings from high-rise buildings. It was impossible to get your bearings from the winds in this city, it was built without structures to mark out the north, but also without any to designate south, west, and east, all the buildings were alike in their layout and shape, all of them smelled the same and rumbled the same, even the squares, intersections, streets, and parks imitated each other, he was very cautious about winds, almost indifferent, he couldn't warm to the thought of them, north and south were as irrelevant to him as east and west. Probably the winds themselves were at fault for that, since they constantly eluded his fingernails and he couldn't scratch his way to the heart of them. No, Tjaž didn't like winds, couldn't warm up to any of them, and if he had been forced to care for one, he wouldn't have known what to do with it, he couldn't rely on them, they didn't strike him as distinctive enough, it could easily happen that someone who meant to go north wound up going east. Instead of appealing to him, they upset him. Let's assume that an individual is in location X. Someone who comes toward him from the north has to catch sight of him to the south, someone who tracks him from behind would see him to the north, and whoever approached location X from the east would have to come to the conclusion that it's located west of him, and whoever is positioned to the west would see point X in the east. The steel horseflies that had ingested bombs in the north and belched them out in the south hadn't left any scratches or scars running from north to south, as you would have assumed from their flight paths, instead they pitched them out all over the city, this way and that, a little here, a little there, a bit more damage here, a little less there. It was the same with the sun, usually the sun came up from behind a peak or over a wasteland and went down in a beech grove or a lake, as long as nothing more attractive forced it to go down someplace else. Here it was impossible to limit or fix the movements of the sun to a particular path, here the sun rose and set past chimneys, it moved past numerous buildings quite simply, and somewhere in the midst of them past numerous houses, sometimes even over them, under them, in front of or behind them, which permitted the conclusion that one was dealing with a very dynamic and particular sun. These circumstances even simplified the sunrises and sunsets, because the sun didn't have to seek out a suitable landing place on the horizon, all it had to do was roll behind some high walls toward the cellars and sink in the coal and potatoes, then in the morning claw its way up over the beer casks and crates of turnips and cabbage. It took off through the streets and roads, or that's how I picture it, lingering a bit here and a bit there, it went faster one minute and slower the next, heading out straight and then going in zigzags, aiming in one direction, but then flying off in another. He sat on a bench and leaned against a poplar, or that's how I picture it, switched the poplar for a chestnut tree, the crossroads for a stoplight, a ditch for a display window. What else should he have done, what can you do on the first day of the second day's freedom, a person's not fit for intelligent work, isn't receptive to other tasks. He retched windows into the walls and fences, that's how I imagine it, sweated roads and squares, pooped fences and railings, scratched points onto signposts, strangled the striking of clocks, stabbed sidewalks, persuaded his stomach, pinched off a crumb of bread, swallowed the racket and shouting, exhausted travelers' eyes, whistled embracing bodies apart, did we do this yet, we haven't done this yet, so he whistled embracing bodies apart, retched roads and squares, sweated fences and railings, pooped points onto directional signs, scratched out the striking of clocks, strangled sidewalks, stabbed his stomach, persuaded a crumb of bread, pinched off the racket and shouting, swallowed travelers' eyes, exhausted bodies embracing, whistled the windows in walls and fences apart, sweated the points onto signposts, pooped on the striking of clocks, scratched out sidewalks, strangled his stomach, stabbed a crumb of bread, persuaded the racket and shouting, pinched off travelers' eyes, swallowed bodies embracing, exhausted the windows in walls and fences, whistled the roads and squares apart, retched fences and railings, pooped on the sidewalks, scratched out his stomach, strangled a crumb of bread, stabbed the racket and shouting, persuaded travelers' eyes, pinched off bodies embracing, swallowed windows in walls and fences, exhausted the roads and squares, whistled fences and railings apart, retched the points of signposts, sweated the striking of clocks, scratched out crumbs of bread, strangled the racket and shouting, stabbed travelers' eyes, persuaded bodies embracing, pinched off the windows in walls and fences, swallowed roads and squares, exhausted fences and railings, whistled the points of signposts apart, retched the striking of clocks, sweated sidewalks, pooped out his stomach, strangled travelers' eyes, stabbed bodies embracing, persuaded the windows in walls and fences, pinched off roads and squares, swallowed fences and railings, exhausted the points on signposts, whistled the striking of clocks apart, retched sidewalks, sweated his stomach, pooped out a crumb of bread, scratched out the racket and shouting, stabbed the windows in the walls and fences, persuaded the roads and squares, pinched off the fences and railings, swallowed the points off of signposts, exhausted the striking of clocks, whistled sidewalks apart, retched his stomach, sweated a crumb of bread, pooped out the racket and shouting, scratched out travelers' eyes, strangled bodies embracing, persuaded fences and railings, pinched the points off of signposts, swallowed the striking of clocks, exhausted sidewalks, whistled his stomach apart, retched a crumb of bread, sweated the racket and shouting, pooped out travelers' eyes, scratched out bodies embracing, strangled windows in the walls and fences, stabbed roads and squares, pinched off the striking of clocks, swallowed sidewalks, exhausted his stomach, whistled a crumb of bread apart, retched the racket and shouting, sweated travelers' eyes, pooped out bodies embracing, scratched out windows in walls and fences, strangled roads and squares, stabbed fences and railings, persuaded the points of signposts, swallowed his stomach, exhausted a crumb of bread, whistled the racket and shouting apart, retched travelers' eyes, sweated bodies embracing, pooped out windows in walls and fences, scratched out roads and squares, strangled fences and railings, stabbed the points of signposts, persuaded the striking of clocks, pinched off sidewalks, exhausted the racket and shouting, whistled travelers' eyes apart, retched bodies embracing, sweated windows in walls and fences, pooped out roads and squares, scratched out fences and railings, strangled the points of signposts, stabbed the striking of clocks, persuaded the sidewalks, pinched off his stomach, swallowed a crumb of bread, tracked down a boy with a slingshot. Up to that point he hadn't been able to imagine a boy with a slingshot, although he had been trying to imagine him all those years, nobody at the institution had ever promised him: tomorrow we'll go see the boy with the slingshot. His father could have introduced him to the world of slingshots, but he had more than enough work to do in the forest, and after that on the roads, he felled trees from morning to night, his hands had grown used to axes, hooks, and draw knives, his son's soft little paw wasn't a match for the father's hard hands, or for a slingshot, and I can't say why it never occurred to Tjaž that he could make them himself, and that's why slingshots never turned up in his childhood. Now he had suddenly chanced on his first one, he had run into a boy roaming around town with a slingshot. When he first caught sight of him, he wasn't roaming around town with a slingshot, he was in a playground walking right up next to a wall where lizards had been waging a fierce battle with the children, but before that the boy must have been roaming around town with his slingshot, and that must have been strange. There were lots of children on the playground and just as many trees, not quite as many benches, and in the middle there was a fishpond with no fish in it, so there was no fishpond in the middle. There was lots of sand scattered around and the mothers were introducing their little ones to sand. There were lots of things to play on and the mothers were introducing their little ones to the things to play on, what else should they have been introducing them to, there were no fathers around, and that was an absence you could see in the children. The mothers sat around on the benches, ready at any moment to separate their little ones from other little ones or to extricate their little ones from the things to play on, if necessary. Whenever they took their little ones away from other little ones or extracted their little ones from the things to play on, they would wave their arms, and they did that with such intensity that it sapped all their breath. They didn't shout at the boy with the slingshot and Tjaž connected that with the slingshot, nobody else had one except this boy and no mother called him, because he had a slingshot, there was something domineering and dangerous about that weapon. Nor did the boy ever go running off to the benches where the mothers sat and kept watch over their little ones, because the slingshot kept him from that, all of the others went there at least enough to get sand all over their mothers' dresses. When Tjaž was sure that he could sit here undisturbed and kill an hour or two, he set his luggage down by the wall and stretched out in the grass next to a steam shovel. It was a big steam shovel made out of red plastic, with outsized wheels and a long arm with a scoop on the end. Barely had Tjaž sat down when the boy with the slingshot shouted, his voice rising up brightly over the other voices, and at first it wasn't clear who he was aiming his voice at, it could have been the mothers for refusing to shout at him, or it could have been the sand or the fishpond or the trees or the red steam shovel. Even as he shouted he picked up his bow, aimed, and hit Tjaž in the leg, planting a quick pain in it that pushed in deeper, toward the bone, and this sufficed for Tjaž to pick himself up, hitch into his luggage and run alongside the wall toward the edge of the playground. Once he was out on the sidewalk he pulled his trouser leg up to pluck out the pain under his knee before it could spread to his other limbs, but it was too late, because his chatty blood had already apportioned the pain. He found himself in front of a high wooden fence that apparently served various authorities as a bulletin board, there were all sorts of posters hanging on it that differed in color, shape, content, and age, that had no other purpose or ambition than to differ in color, shape, content, and age, and differ they did, exhaustively, mind-numbingly, to the very last one, because there was otherwise no difference between them. Tjaž decided that he would devote the rest of the time available to him on this first free day to the posters. His fingernails had started to itch and he missed those heavy Swedish printing presses, how long had it been since he tangled with them. In the meantime they'd bought new ones and they were producing a new generation of posters with them, which they were committing to walls, billboards, and fences. Advertise on local fences, thank you, you won't regret it, you'll see the difference it makes. Tjaž examined the announcements, advertisements, invitations, and news postings that even the worst weather couldn't undermine, he examined all of them and gave thought to each one separately, there sure were a lot of people who advertised on this fence. Suddenly a big dog appeared in front of the bulletin board, whether it was there before Tjaž or Tjaž before it is unclear, perhaps it just crawled up out of the ground or came from behind the fence, I don't know, it just appeared silently, suddenly it was there and Tjaž noticed it when it was already standing right beside him. He had to act quickly, prepare for their meeting, show himself to be friendly. Tjaž recalled all the dog breeds that a boarding school student can possibly recollect in that short a time and, more out of caution than conviction, categorized this dog as a German shepherd. That was at least something, even if not much in this unanticipated and dangerous moment, Tjaž acted more out of some instinct that dictated "better to aim too high than too low." The German shepherd couldn't have cared less about Tjaž's ignorance of the variety of dog breeds, it was drawn to the billboard by other needs. First its eyes moved over Tjaž, then it sniffed at his pant leg and paused for a while over the bruise that the mischievous slingshot had inflicted, then it moved up to his scrotum, which it rubbed its muzzle on for a while, then it tracked down his stalk and with a wag of its tail signaled agreement with it. Through all of this Tjaž didn't dare move, rarely in his life had he stood this still, he didn't resist the dog's being so close, he didn't dare not put up with it as long as the dog kept nudging its cold nose into his scrotum and mussing it up. He sighed in relief when the dog started sniffing the boards, sniffed over all of the planks, rummaged through the posters, and finally decided on one inviting young people to a church social—invited them, nonsense. It was drumming young people out to this social, which is to say that the dog found the poster that most suited its needs, the selection on the billboard was broad and varied, indeed, and it could have chosen some other sheet of paper, but no, it chose the church's youth social, and it didn't take long for it to choose, it found it right off, it extricated that day from among all the other days, sized up its choice, lifted its leg, and let loose its stream, and a German shepherd like that lets loose a stream that really means something, that other streams have to defer to, it rattled the fence and bounced off the planks, this stream gave those fat letters some solid knocks as it rattled over the paper, while the dog stood on three legs, sticking its tongue out at Tjaž. Tjaž understood this language of out-thrust tongue and thundering stream. Suddenly the dog adjusted its footing by shifting its legs and releasing what was left of the stream from the other side, it took aim at the theatrical troupe that was going to perform some little skit, it sprayed the dancers, sprayed the band and the little choruses that had their performances ahead of them, and finally it soaked the speakers with a fine, silken spray. Tjaž began to form a serious assessment of this dog that was by no means negative, he fully approved the dog's selections, he liked it, and it wouldn't have taken much for him to call it, to adopt it as his own, come with me, and the dog would have obeyed, two homeless souls would have continued their journey together. Instinct told him not to do that, however, and Tjaž put a lot of stock in instinct. From that point on Tjaž's path can be traced almost uninterruptedly. Right after the poster where the German shepherd relieved itself, he must have thought of the skyscraper café and at the same time remembered his fingernails. The institution had weaned him, there was no question about that, it had aged and disowned him, and from then on he would have to fend for himself, from then on he would welcome anything that lightened his load as he fought his way through freedom. Traveling had worn him out, he had spent the whole day wandering aimlessly around town. For a while he sat on a bench about which he knew nothing more than that it was a bench that felt good, that soothed his exhausted limbs, which had done their share of walking, nothing else about the bench interested him. He asked the clock in a nearby bell tower for the time, and since it had plenty, it parted with a bushel, ringing at ten. They close the skyscraper café at midnight, so he's taken care of for the next two hours. He entered the elevator and pleaded for a minute or two, that wasn't much, but Tjaž was grateful to it and once at the top stepped out of it convivially. There weren't many people in the café, the evening was favorable, what am I saying favorable, the evening was made for him. From the terrace you could see over the whole city and far out beyond it, its fluttering glow reached all the way up to his feet, his eyes looked for a path into the wavering light, he could see Nini's room and the lights of the boarding school. The city squinted in the transparent glow, some lights out on the edge of town were already going out or getting covered in twilight that thickened into darkness, a wind whistled in from the mountains and forests, its whistle winding past ears and tossing the laundry that hung in courtyards and on balconies up in the air. At this hour the distance between trees and people got shorter until they merged into one, the distinction vanished, people were trees and trees were people and dwelled among us. At this time the streets were empty and there were no people on the sidewalks, life turned around and flowed elsewhere. This was all right with Tjaž, it would have been irresponsible to threaten their heads needlessly with falling shards. This was the most favorable moment. Tjaž leaned on the terrace, felt his way to Nini's window, rapping lightly with the knuckles of his right hand on the pane of glass, rapping ever so lightly and considerately, the way a storm bubbles and asks for permission to open its sluices, to open them and dump all this water on the earth. Everyone knows that you have to accommodate storms. Tjaž was rapping very considerately on Nini's window, signaling to her that she needed to understand, that she should get to safety, a sliver of glass pane might gain independence, find a way through the curtain and fly into her eye. He had spent a lot of time introducing her to his craft, getting her used to taking precautions, trying to work as much understanding out of her as he could, teaching her the basic methods of scratching and taking her along with him to particularly instructive performances, and now it was time to see if any of that had sunk in. She'd better not forget that she, too, is always vulnerable to him, she'd better not put on any airs, better not let them lead her to do something stupid. For now she just had to get someplace safe, he couldn't warn her of the danger any more clearly, he can't wait any longer, his nails have already taken the window as a target and he's begun to drum more insistently on the pane. Now he was drumming very hard and the window began baring itself, his nails sank into the glass up to the skin and then pulled: down twice, then twice across, they crushed the glass, putty and all, right out of the window frame and finally ground the glass from both windows down into bits. It flew onto the sidewalk and street, ringing and chattering on the hard asphalt, each sliver of pane jingling separately and echoing back up to the top of the skyscraper. With this maneuver he had set aside his usual method and instead emulated a glazier, which is to say that in dismantling the glass he held precisely to the sequence that the glazier had used when installing it. Before Tjaž ordered his nails to pierce the curtains, to break into her room, he popped the last bits of glass, the ones that remained stuck in the putty after the first attack or had resisted for other reasons, out of the window frames—that is to say, he popped out the last, resistant remains of the panes before slashing the empty window squares to ribbons. Now his nails could attack the room unimpeded, the curtains yielding and permitting a clear view of the room. Nini was lying under a blanket, where she had stopped leafing through some magazine without yet having realized what was happening to her window, when Tjaž flew through the space in passing to satisfy himself that she was alone in the room, that struck him as an important precaution to take in any event, because somebody else could have been there and trying his stalk out with her. Tjaž's nails would have dispelled that pleasure for him, there's no doubt about that, but there was no need. Once he was sure that she was alone in the room, he popped a finger at the lightbulb that shone on her nightstand, then at the one at the ceiling that welcomed him from under a big lampshade, and both of them succumbed to his nails with a bright zzzzip, the room sank into complete darkness, and a fat breeze smirked in through the disrobed windows. Tjaž's nails returned to the terrace of the skyscraper café. Barely a few minutes had passed by the time they returned, the whole business had taken less time than comparable things take in novels. The night had moved forward by barely an inch.

6.

A CHAPTER ABOUT
MULTIPLYING CHAIRS

The black spider that appeared on the ceiling wasn't actually black—that is, its bottom part was black, its belly and between its legs, but that side of it couldn't be seen because it faced the ceiling. So what Tjaž saw on the ceiling wasn't actually a spider, although by all means it could have been a spider, but rather a spider's back, which in fact wasn't black, but green, except that this color was so modestly expressed that it's hardly worth mentioning, and ultimately the spider's green back appeared to be the same black color as its belly actually was. Have I distinguished the color of the spider's belly from the color of the spider's back clearly enough, I believe so, have I also said that the spider's back didn't tolerate black, I need to add that. It's not worth wasting any breath over the size and shape of the spider, so I won't talk about that, as much as I'd like to. And that's a shame. At any rate, Tjaž wasn't bothered by the colors of the spider's belly and back, but rather the fact that till now he had not ascribed this animal any more influence than the spinning of webs, hunting for fleas, and sucking of blood, he was behind in his thinking about it, he hadn't advanced his relationship to spiders as far as he should have, until now they'd caused him no trouble, but also no pleasantness, so he hadn't really been inspired by his relationship to them, and now this had begun to disturb him and awaken a sense of guilt. This spider had its intentions, it was plotting something, there was no doubt about that, it was baying openly at him, it was quite intentional, it ought to be locked up in a zoo. Never before would it have occurred to him to take an interest in bugs on the ceiling, they showed up everywhere, on every ceiling and wall and in every corner, even at the institution and in Nini's room, but now he felt threatened and his instinct told him to protect himself on all sides from anything that could impinge on him in any possible way, and this meant protecting himself from the café spider, and that wouldn't be bad, because he was certain it was the only spider in the café, which made it an exceptional, isolated case. It's true that the black spider had begun to oppress him, his first day in freedom could wind up putting him in danger, all the spider needed to do was put its hydraulics in gear and a rope would begin to unravel and carry it from the ceiling down into the room, and as it descended it would get closer and closer to Tjaž's neck and there it would drill toward his pith. Tjaž could avoid this attack by retreating somewhere else, to the next table or another corner, but this sort of retreat struck him as being against his nature, it was paltry stuff, not worthy of him, and why it wasn't should be perfectly clear if I remind you that this is the kid who had de-shoed a fellow student, flayed two or three men's backs, lacerated some saints, wrecked an altar scaffold, demolished a printing press, just now commended the panes in Nini's room to the beyond, scratched out her window, stripped out its panes, popped the glass off the lightbulbs, dismissed the putty from the window frames, deprived Nini of her magazine and her night, forced her to undertake certain chores that she wouldn't have been caught dead doing under other circumstances, for any amount of money, but that she now had to do regardless, look for the electrical outlet and her slippers under the bed, the door handle, key, doorway, and hall, and all of them in first-rate darkness, in the hallway look for the fuse box and, inside it, look for the fuse that caused the darkness of which she accused them all more and more harshly and bitterly, but incorrectly, finally mustering the courage to stick her long fingers inside, unscrew a first fuse and screw it back in, unscrew a second fuse and screw it back in, unscrew a third fuse and screw it back in, none of which helped, the light didn't go on, the fuses were all fine and couldn't shriek it back on for her, they weren't at fault for the darkness, but something must be at fault for the darkness, a short while before it was still light in her room, how else could she have leafed through her magazine, how else could Tjaž have found her window in the night, suddenly there had been the sound of glass shattering, the lights went into eclipse, eaten by void, so that she had no choice but to resort to the fuse box and tell them about the dark, which was superfluous, a completely erroneous, even decadent assumption. That was the crux of it, given all this it wasn't appropriate to flee a spider dragging its rope behind it down into the room, a spider that, moreover, had only dropped about an inch from the ceiling. Tjaž stayed where he was, as was only fitting, he immersed himself in the spider's landing and prepared himself for their meeting. He watched how the spider slowly drew the ceiling behind it down into the room, the ceiling pressing down on the rope, the rope on the spider, the spider on the column of air between it and Tjaž, the air on Tjaž's body, his body on the chair, the chair on the floor, the floor on the ceiling of the next level down, the floor of that level on the ceiling of the next level down, the ceiling of that level on the floor of the same level, the floor of that level on the ceiling of the next level down, the ceiling of that level on the floor of the same level, the floor of that level on the ceiling of the next level down, the ceiling of that level on the floor of the same level, and so on, all the way down, lower and lower, floor after floor into the depths, down to the ground floor, the ceilings pressing down on the floors and the floors pressing down on the ceilings beneath them, through all the levels down to the ground floor, where the ground floor pressed down on the basement, and it pressed down on the parcel of land that the skyscraper was built on. At first glance the spider hanging down from the ceiling of the skyscraper café and coincidentally aiming for Tjaž's head was an insignificant little shadow or at most a stain that had survived spring cleaning, nothing to get excited about, nothing dangerous, most likely just some trifle that didn't deserve the least attention, but because this little creature was dragging the ceiling behind it down into the room and thus was exerting pressure on the whole skyscraper, through all its ceilings and floors down to its roots, did I say roots, down to its foundations, I have to say that the matter was grave indeed. But that wasn't even the whole story. While the floors pressed down from top to bottom, which is to say vertically, into the depths, the basement pressed outward, apart, horizontally, seeking breadth, the skyscraper's basement pressed on the basements of the neighboring buildings, the neighboring basements pressed on the streets and squares—on these, of course, more from below than laterally—then after that on still other basements, and at this point not just in one, but in several directions, so that some five or six basements and some four or five roads pressed on Tjaž's boarding school too. It was getting on toward midnight, just a few more minutes and Tjaž would conclude his first day of freedom and begin a new one, he would start his second day of freedom in the year one after Tjaž, the buckets, brushes, rags, pails, and detergent, the walk through the town, the stream of that dog, the shattered panes of Nini's window and all the other exertions of this day had been necessary for him to thoroughly forget, break free of the institution, evade its tightest bonds, air out his walls, equalize the psychological pressure that comes about with a change of atmosphere, he had already run through so many crucial things that were bound to come between him and the institution, to polarize and estrange them one from the other, and here a little spider like this on the café ceiling upends all the work he'd accomplished, voids and invalidates it, crosses it out, turns it inside out, and changes it however it pleases, reestablishes ties you don't want, chases the new off and brings back the old. That institution clings to you like a bedbug, you can't overpower it, you don't touch it, yet it touches you, it won't let go, won't give back your soul, it dances around and teases you or swings its billy club over your head while you're forever on the verge of giving up the ghost at last but can't ever get it over with because the club doesn't hit hard enough, you can't squeeze the worm-eaten life out of your body, it sticks to you for better or worse, you shove it away but can't depart, you're condemned to hang around, to dawdle, until at last the dawdling itself gives it new life in some other place. Again your spine stoops, your legs straighten out, and your hands clasp together as before, once again your suit soaks in the walls, the wood, the paper, the rules, superiors, and overseers and all the other components that are the pride and joy of the people, the familiar, threadbare drudgery of old sucks you back in, you grab onto it without being able to tell the different tasks apart, you hitch into all of them at once, and in that at least you find a kind of difference, since before you only experienced one task at a time, individually, each one deliberately and on its own, but now you experience them all clumped together and simplified, all merged into a single, unified task, and of course it strikes you in the process that this or that dominates, for instance one day the dining room exuding soups with unaltered haste, though soup isn't the main course, the whole dining room smells of them, it never smells of the main course, the smell of it never sticks, never asserts itself, the soups continually drive it out, outshout it, occupy all strategic positions and man the choke points, and that's why soups get stressed so much and why the main course always gets neglected. Or let's take another picture, morning at the institution, morning revolves around the underpants that with bashful cautiousness, and sometimes right under the covers, trade places with the pajamas, then after that, sooner or later, morning revolves around soap, toothpaste, prayers, folkways, and customs, then in the evening student life focuses on the toilets, where the boys shove, elbow, and prod their way toward regimenting their excretions. Even the waitress to some extent can pick up the scent of your institutional past, which is to be inferred from the provocative, almost mocking way she set glasses down and carried bottles away, the way she reached over the table, the way she swayed her hips and shook her breasts as she walked, and the way he crept out of his past into her, all these things led him to conclude that he would soon put the institution behind him after all. At these moments the spiderwebs made him an old boarding school boy again with all the virtues and rectitude thereof, and this despite the fact that he spent all day straining and killing himself to abolish those ties. Apparently this smell he was spreading appealed to the waitress, arousing her, with regard to him anyway, although it was impossible to judge just what about him drew her to him. He pictured himself on a horse, for the first time testing his nails as a sovereign scratcher, and they obeyed him. Nini's vacated window clearly attested to that. His scratching abilities were not bound to his chosen profession, much less to any particular social condition, to any particular place or particular climate, not in the slightest, he would be free to create, and what was decisive was his personal, inner relationship to whatever thing he set his sights on scratching to bits. The encounter with the German shepherd in front of the billboard may have been unpleasant, but in fact it was his first free test of the toughness he had developed during his time at the institution, for instance by acquainting the whole assembled church with his sleeping habits. The visits at Nini's had been useful to sharpen his scratching sense, which allowed him to foresee and sometimes even determine the outcomes and success of his scratchings. It was in the skyscraper café that he first tried scratching long-distance and perfected his approach and technique, and most of all improved his aim, taking into account that he performed his first scratch from a distance of barely a foot and a half away—at a time, of course, when he was just a poor, unproven beginner—but now his nails could function flawlessly at a distance of several kilometers. All the scratching sprees recounted so far and others like them made it possible for him to get faster as well, so that subsequently he had several levels of speed to choose from, and they made it possible for him to aim his nails more accurately still, to escalate the scratches and extract every last spasm from them, then grant them some hard-earned attention and rest, reward them for a job well done, but the most priceless achievement of all was that he'd learned how to properly assess the situation before and after a job—in other words, to determine beforehand whether he should go for an attack, an assault, or a blitz, and whether or not a normal grip would suffice, a light and simple swipe, just a swat, so to say, in passing. After the job was completed he knew just how much practice would be needed to correct his errors and deficiencies, smooth out any awkwardness, improve his technique—in a word—to raise his agility to just the desired level of acuity. In view of these exalted notions Tjaž justifiably had an exalted opinion of himself, which ought not to have veered off into arrogance or conceit, but in fact did veer in just that direction. It was precisely at this intersection of facts and rashness that the spider appeared, a little creature that at first glance should in no way have influenced Tjaž's disposition, but in fact went well beyond influencing to damage and wreck it. And here it becomes like any other boarding school story, Tjaž had sinned, even if only a bit, he had permitted himself really just the tiniest sin, but it had earned him a punishment, because he shouldn't have permitted himself any sin at all. It had earned him a punishment, because in both this world and the beyond not a single hair goes uncounted, much less a sin, and I see that instead of Tjaž I've begun to speak about god and his habit of punishing sins. We have to talk about him, I certainly think so, he deserves it, depends on it, he gets no respect—a pity—goes unknown, or, rather, he's known only as much as he's talked about, and that isn't much, people run out of things to say pretty quickly, or he gets talked about a lot without anything actually being said, which is understandable, because he's more or less from the gutter, a creature from society's lower strata, and on top of that such an unfortunate name attesting to his modest, dubious past, related as it is to the words clod, sod, odd, which all suggest something dirt poor, deprived, it belongs to that family, wait, related how, hold on, it's on the tip of my tongue, I don't know, did I ever know, I seem to recall that I never needed to know that before. Now I still say thank god about the spider, because that's the same as if I were talking about Tjaž, while I've thankfully stopped talking about god and how dirt poor he is. Why I stopped talking about him precisely at this point, more about that later, if we have occasion and time, perhaps in the autumn or better yet in the winter when we'll see what kind of fall and what kind of winter we're going to have, last year's was brutal, and it looks like this year's will be, but forget about that, I would really like for us never again to fall silent about the spider, it should be talked about extensively and at length, talked about through and through, up and down and all around and every blue moon of the year, we've kept quiet about it for too long, neglected it, and maybe an intolerant soul here and there has even hated it, but anyway, it doesn't matter what I talked about before, because I'm going to have to talk about it again later, even though I'm already talking about it now. As far as I was concerned, to the extent it was in my power, immediately, at the first sign, just as soon as they banged that shovel as a sign for me to start, I began, I began describing Tjaž. I've been describing him using Pontius Pilate pencils, if I'm not mistaken, I have a bunch of them in a glass, would you like some statistical data, you wouldn't, it's enough if I like them, there's a good fistful of them, that should suffice, though god knows my fist isn't all that big, and I even doubt whether it's at all adequate, I've certainly seen better fists, my fist pales in comparison with them, but until I find some other unit of measure, I'll stick to my own fist, principle is my system, system is my principle, for the moment my fist is the best dry unit of measure of all that I've yet applied to picking up pencils, for the moment it meets my needs, I can't complain, what it will be like later I can't say, I've always got it on me, it comes in handy, I won't try to hide the fact that for practical reasons, precisely because of the Pontius Pilates I use to describe Tjaž, the pencil points stare up at the ceiling, uniformity suits them very well, they're used to it, I take them out of the glass and describe Tjaž, the lines stretching into the distance, my pencils are a durable brand, a regular cornfield, and my manuscript is a regular silo. Before I began my description I sharpened all of my pencils so I wouldn't have to sharpen them in the midst of describing something, because sharpening pencils entertains me too much, right away too many colors and patterns distract me from work, otherwise we're perfectly compatible, each one gets its turn to contribute a few sentences, I'm not all that demanding, but I do have some minimum expectations, and then I'm satisfied and the pages of this small accounting ledger slowly fill up while the pencils grow dull and their points become fat. I have to stop, there's no way around it, reach for the sharpener and plane away at my Pontius Pilates in their glass, retaper their tips, permit myself a little downtime, in fact, offer myself a cigarette then politely refuse it, thanks, I don't smoke, and anyway there isn't a cigarette in the house, there isn't a match in the house, there isn't an ashtray in the house, there isn't a jar lid in the house, there aren't any and never have been, so my offer of a cigarette to myself is just a formality, a courtesy, an empty gesture, lacking in serious intent, made more or less for a change, as a diversion, and that's important too, because all this Tjažing along is fatiguing and this story is very exhausting work. All the components of my story about Tjaž that I've enumerated here are inextricably interlinked, and it's my story only to the extent I'm developing it, and not because I experienced it in my own skin or because I continue to experience it, which certain ideologues are bound to accuse me of, because that way it's easier for them to peck at me, but otherwise the thought doesn't occur to me that anybody might identify this story with the details of my curriculum vitae, my professional employment in the bureau of reports naturally encourages that sort of identification, even forces that sort of impression, and here every denial will fall on deaf ears, even the solemn assurances of my boss, the one for whom I work, who knows me in detail like few other people, otherwise I couldn't work for him, whose initiative this story about Tjaž is, who launched and commissioned this whole business and decided to burden me with this report, why me of all people and not some other employee, because, you see, my life lacked and continues to lack any similarity at all with Tjaž's life, that's why he assigned this work to me and nobody else, only I will be able to report on Tjaž in an unprejudiced way, or so says my boss, but who will believe that, and that's why my boss's assurances landed on deaf ears, but that doesn't count for much, and let me just add that my agency takes on only obscure, exceptional, and marginal cases, which—counter to all expectations—have been growing more frequent among the people, leading our agency to recruit a whole slew of new employees, which naturally has no impact on this story, because I took on Tjaž's case before that and the other employees are busy with other assignments and I have to come up with all this material on my own, unassisted, so that the report will be as factual and documentarily precise as possible. I like my profession and take it seriously, and not just because it's my daily bread, I can say that my profession brings me joy, if you will. I took on Tjaž's case, with all the rights and privileges, so that after my reprimand for this break I return to the starting point, to the skyscraper café. The basement of the boarding school soon absorbed the pressure that began with the café's spider, and the basement immediately began to return it, because pressure like that cannot and must not go without a response, there are regulations and clauses, and I've been reminded of them again and again, this is your duty, you're honor-bound, wash your hands in innocence in front of the crowd, the measures you've taken have always been the right ones, let everyone see that you're enacting the law to the letter, with such precision, you can't allow every cripple to throw shit in your face, not even in your imagination can you allow such feces to stick to you, so any pressure like that must not go unanswered, you've got to knock the scum down before it spreads, so that's why the institution's basement pushed back very hard through the whole suburb all the way to the skyscraper's basement, and the skyscraper's basement pushed even harder against the ground floor, and the ground floor pushed with incredible force against the first floor, the first floor against the second, the second against the third and so on, higher and higher, up to the floor of the café, where the floor pressed on Tjaž's chair, and the chair pressed on Tjaž's ass, on his scrotum and the bottom of his thighs, trying to press against his ass just as forcefully as it pressed against his scrotum and thighs. That's where the pressure got stuck, it didn't press any farther—against his lungs, stomach, appendix, intestines, kidneys, or heart, for instance, where it could have pressed to its heart's content, it seemed wholly uninterested in pressing outward, forward, or backward, up or down, out or in or anywhere, it just pressed right where it was, into itself, in and of itself, so to speak, and from that Tjaž could discern the very everyday form that the pressure had taken, it was a simple round little ball, the tiniest dough ball that was unusual only to the extent that dough could be unusual to anybody.

Tjaž's stomach ached whenever the little ball pressed, he could also have had an ache somewhere else, but let's be modest and humble, let's make do with a stomach ache, the stomach aches easiest of all, the simplest most fundamentally straightforward aches are in the stomach, so let's let Tjaž's stomach ache, as long as something has to, it's agreed. Tjaž grabbed his stomach, it was stabbing him, first with his right hand, then with his left hand, minding the sequence, so that the right hand was engaged with his stomach just as many times as the left, and for that reason he switched hands at equal intervals. As the waitress, for instance, was adding up the bill for the next table, for two longhaired youths, his right hand had just finished stomach duty and had to yield the stomach to his left hand before the waitress even finished with the bill. She was standing just beside his table—this is the waitress I'm referring to—listening to the youths itemize their visit and pushing her pencil over the paper so her breasts shook as they jutted centrifugally out from her body, offering themselves to view. Tjaž no longer tried to conceal where he was looking, he was having to deal with the dough in his stomach and the changing of the hands, which were no longer taming the ball of dough, but were operating out of his left pocket, where they had to maneuver his stalk, which had since expanded and got caught in his underwear, into an appropriate pose, which is to say into his left pant leg, where on occasions like this, when it expanded, it had its own special nook, and there it decidedly drove out the bread ball. At that point the absolutely crazy idea flashed through Tjaž's head of taking some object, for example a glass, an ashtray or a vase, and setting it on the waitress's breasts. There are days when very little or virtually nothing happens, and then there are days, for instance today, that are full of surprises great and small, when new scenes are continually bubbling up before a person's eyes with no end in sight, you can't bring the day to a conclusion, and similarly the report on Tjaž doesn't require a conclusion, there is no conclusion expected, I don't have to conclude the day with a particular word of any particular content, or with some special bit of punctuation, a comma let's say, a question mark, an exclamation point or a semicolon, or with some particular act or at curfew or closing time, what do you think, not at all, not without boasting or making a big deal of myself, and I really don't need to do that, I can end the day where I like, I can shorten it by several hours or draw it out to my heart's content, that's up to me, the head of the reporting service knows that his best instructions to me are the ones that he doesn't give. In this case I don't have to check against any standards, I can just leave an event out, or I can include it and organize it into chapters and paragraphs, begin it with roman numerals then shift to Arabic ones and draw on all other halfway sensible alphabets, I can add footnotes if I like, that's up to me, don't interfere in my business, please, you don't have a right to go poking your nose in, I can reject an incident, if I like, and prefer some other, I can mark a particular incident as crucial, even if maybe it isn't, or I can quite simply overlook some other incident, even though it may be crucial, all of these options are left up to me, though of course for the sake of the cause I'll see to it that I don't overlook or omit any incident. If I got held up with the German shepherd for quite a while and let its stream thunder onto the poster on the bulletin board or its muzzle muss up Tjaž's scrotum, believe me when I say I had reasons for doing that, or if I lingered on Tjaž's desire to set a glass, ashtray, or vase on the waitress's breasts, and if on the other hand I completely neglected Tjaž's final meeting with those in charge before he left the boarding school, then there are reasons for that too, and I've thought about what those reasons might be, and I think it's because the first type of incidents originated with Tjaž, while those of the second type didn't. Perhaps there are some other reasons at work here, but I don't remember them, nor will I remember them later, they'll never occur to me, that's been decided. Tjaž's stalk had finished roaming the length of his left pants leg, the two longhairs had left, disappeared in the elevator, the café had emptied out, the lights over the emptied tables were going out, the waitress was shutting away the coffees and teas, the beers and vermouths, the cognacs and champagnes, the lemonades and aperitifs, she had begun putting away the glasses and bottles and cups and utensils, locking them up, subordinating them to herself and putting them safely out of reach, she began wiping the bar and the tables down and flicking the switches, prompting the lights to go out. Soon the last ray of light bit the dust and pitch darkness came calling, good evening, how goes it. This ambiance sat well with him, the little ball stopped roaming through Tjaž's stomach, settled in his lower body, found a spot for itself, and calmed down. He figured he was going to have to spend the night somewhere and somehow, arrange a place to sleep for himself, maybe he would sleep right at the table or on some chairs, he would have to set up the chairs in two rows, let's say five chairs per row to obtain a surface of ten chairs, you could sleep comfortably on a surface like that, ten chairs would suffice, he could set all ten chairs in a single row or one over the other, vertically, stacking them up toward the ceiling, that would be another possible arrangement, he would have to think about that and consult with the waitress, she would know what the best fit for a person would be, or he could just as easily take all ten chairs and arrange them all around the café, the first one here, the second one there, the third one somewhere else, this one a bit closer, that one farther off, and so on, then he would have to adjust his night's sleep to this, which is to say he would have to move from chair to chair and on each of them spend a certain length of time, which would have to be calculated so that an equal amount of time was allocated to each chair: from twelve to one he would sit on the first chair, from one to two he would sit on the second, from three to four he would sit on the third, and so on up to the last chair, whose turn would come from nine to ten in the morning, which for reasons of time and due to the early opening hours kept by cafés would have been impractical. He had to change over to shorter units of time, he would only be able to allocate a half hour of sleep to each chair, so the time from twelve to twelve thirty for the first one, the time from twelve thirty to one for the second one, the time from one to one thirty for the third one, the time from one thirty to two for the fourth one, and so on until his sleep would be interrupted on the tenth chair at five in the morning, that would work, but he would also have to account for the time it would take him to walk, or rather, to shift from chair to chair, which meant that the night would have to end shortly past five, assuming he didn't choose each subsequent chair according to some special set of rules, but just moved from each to the next in sequence. This procedure, based on time units of a half hour, would have been in complete accord with Tjaž's notions of his first night's sleep in freedom, if only he didn't have to be mindful of the chairs' sequence, because the shifting from chair to chair would have to be ordered so that an equal number of sittings fell to each chair—each chair would serve as first chair just once and as last chair just once, and similarly each would serve as second chair just once, as third chair just once, as fourth, fifth, sixth, seventh, eighth, and ninth chair just once. This could be accomplished in one of two ways. The first way would be to start out each time sitting at one end of the café, and in this case he would have to keep shifting the chairs and arranging them so that each time a new chair was in first place, and a new chair was in second place, and a new chair was in third place, and so on until the last possible arrangement was exhausted and at the next shift the options would have to repeat again from the beginning. The other way would be for him to leave all the chairs in their places all night long and start out by sitting on a different one each time, so that he would have to sit on each chair ten times, but each time in a different sequence, so that each chair would have its turn, let's say for instance, first as the fifth, then as the sixth, then as the seventh and so on up to tenth and then back to first, so altogether ten times, which would of course also hold for all of the other nine chairs, all ten shifts together would amount to a hundred different sittings before all of the options were exhausted and only at the hundred and first sitting would the first option have to repeat, with each individual sitting lasting at most three to four minutes, regardless of whether the first or the second method was used. Would that be enough, is the seating arrangement sufficiently clear, have we been helpful enough to Tjaž detailing his sleeping arrangements at the top of the skyscraper, have we talked extensively enough about Tjaž's schoolmate and the fate of his shoes, did we dwell long enough on the saints sawed apart, did the beheadings go quickly enough, have we hammered enough sentences into Nini's apartment—still left in the dark—have we lingered sufficiently on the black spider, which wasn't black, or rather was only partly black, but otherwise green, have we also mentioned the sharpener for the pencils I use to describe Tjaž, have we, if only in passing, provided for some new scratch-fest, from the café's terrace it wouldn't be hard to aim at the lights going out in the streets, to crush the lightbulbs and neon tubes with your nails or de-glaze an entire street, it would be worth it to whisk the glass out of display cases, doors, windows, and walls, but why stray like this when there are opportunities so close to home. The chance to sate his nails on the glass in the café and pulverize the bottles, glasses, cups, porcelain bowls, frames, and shelves was enticing, sleep would be a shade sweeter after completing a job like that, but we haven't provided for another scratching. So instead of Tjaž's nails let me talk about how Tjaž tended to the waitress, how he strained and delayed to give her his all, did he succeed, probably so. He spent the night in the café at the top of the skyscraper not on ten chairs, but right on the floor, on the bare linoleum, with the waitress contributing to the extent she was able, helping as much as she could, assisting however was needed. It was at this time, in the first days of the year one after Tjaž, that the spider began unreeling his rope and descending from the ceiling down toward the floor. As it descended it paused, for it had to open its pincers and get them ready, prepare them to chomp, because it couldn't do that while it descended, if only because the descent demanded all of its concentration. When it had opened its pincers and prepared them to chomp, then and only then it descended the last little bit, sized up its target beneath it, landed on the spot it had targeted, sniffed at the sweat and bit.

7.

A CHAPTER ABOUT
WALKING BEHIND ME

On this occasion I'm going to see Tjaž again, with my own eyes, after such a long time I'm going to hear his voice again, smell the perspiration of his skin, listen to the rhythm of his gestures, take in all the elements of his repose, it's a shame that we haven't seen each other in such a long time, my eyes were deaf, we would race past each other without our breaths so much as glancing off each other or our picking up each other's vapors, I had developed no taste for him, of course I could have planted myself outside the door to the institution, waiting for Tjaž, and would have run into him sooner or later, but I didn't, we flowed apart even without our having come from the same source, having flowed jointly through the same river bed or met at a confluence. Institution's door or skyscraper's door, is there a difference, it appears that there isn't, and it may even seem that I'm standing in front of the institution now when in fact I'm standing in front of the skyscraper, or that I'm standing in front of the skyscraper now when in fact I'm standing in front of the institution, that's possible too, you have to take an interest and ask, pardon me, sir, are you familiar with the door I'm standing in front of, thank you for answering, it's not one or the other after all, but some other door and it's not yet quite clear which, it's probably the door of some barracks or the municipal junkyard. I could have stood outside any door in the entire town and Tjaž would have come through it sooner or later, of course I would have had to stand outside any door with the firm intention of Tjaž coming through it and nobody else, you see, even Tjaž sets conditions and makes people worry, there's no hiding it, perhaps that was precisely the reason my relationship to him was so superficial, not to say waspish, we grew estranged from each other and parted ways, him in one direction, me in the other, we had to search each other out anew, what can I say, Tjaž is a victim of my profession, the bureau of reports assigned him to me, I didn't choose him myself, and if I could have I wouldn't have, so I'm not at fault, I'm tracking him on business, out of professional need, chasing after him officially, after all I have to live and have to put clothes on my back too, and it isn't all the same to me how I live and what I wear, for instance now I'm waiting with microphone in hand for Tjaž to come back from the skyscraper café, the highest café in town, so first this, and only afterward food and clothing, the tape recorder is on, the time is right, it's a proper city morning, if that tells you anything and helps you along, the traffic is coming to life, the cars come rumbling out of their garages and later they'll clog up the area around the buildings because there's a shortage of parking spaces, I can hear the drivers who will be cursing, permitting themselves familiar, well-worn curses, like *doggone it* for instance, that's the best curse of all, the cheapest, short and sweet, the most versatile of all the ones we're capable of. At this point there's still some space around the skyscraper because it's still early morning and I've circled the skyscraper two or three times, in the café at the top there were still lights on a while ago, but now they've gone out, if my eyesight serves. Tjaž must have just stepped into the elevator, pressed the button, and started down, till he gets here I'll just have to imagine him, the way he stands in the elevator with his feet spread apart, heading down through all the stories, piercing the floors and ceilings, while at each floor the control panel clicks, it's a long way down, because the café is on the tallest building in town, instead of a cross they fastened a café to its top, it won't be long before the elevator comes to a stop, settles softly onto the ground floor, it won't head down to the basement this early, it will avoid the basement and it's even a question whether the skyscraper was equipped with a basement, I've had my doubts about potatoes, coal, and clutter ever since I've been dealing with Tjaž, I've lost all my faith in rummage and coal and potatoes to boot, heaven help me. At any instant the door will open and I'll see him in front of me for the first time in ages, as I've said, I'll turn on the recorder, hold out the microphone, and I won't have to explain much, it will be enough if I just briefly explain, I'll say we're putting together a complete and accurate picture of him and demolishing the old, distorted one, that we're even going to add some details, attach some embellishments, so to speak, and pretty him up, that we want to make him our own and so on, take him by the arm and so on, that we want to rehabilitate him, and that should be enough, I'm convinced he'll agree down to the last pinch of hay. If necessary, I'll explain all the rest to him as well, I'll underscore the importance of this aspect, touch on the uniqueness of his personality and mention the time crunch that I've been forced into by the bureau of reports, where I'm employed, the phrase bureau of reports will give him a pleasant nudge, it will tickle the soles of his feet and under his chin, it will stroke his honor, and that's important, you have to strike the right chord and he'll be off and ready to climb up onto the tape, Tjaž on tape, everything that came both before and after him and everything that is Tjaž, will be Tjaž, and was Tjaž, all of it will be on tape, what do you suppose the boss will think of that, he'll hug me out of sheer joy that I've delivered Tjaž to him at home, the way I delivered, for instance, a washing machine to his house, got him connected to the electrical grid, hooked into the water line, shoved in a bunch of available underpants and saw to it that the washing machine filled with underpants started its wash cycle, underpants come first, I took care of every task you can imagine, and every task that a new washing machine can endure, and just like that and even better I'll deliver Tjaž to his house, I'll acquire him for him cheap, I'll get him for him almost for free, let's see what he thinks of that. The setting for the recording suits my ideas, I've thought a lot about the best way of putting Tjaž in touch with my bureau and I'm left with the conclusion that I have to put him in touch with it at least as well as I did with the washing machine, the setting is very conducive to success—the street, the cars, the smell of gasoline, the commuters—I'm still working on my questions, so it suits me that Tjaž is taking longer to come down than I expected he would. How he spent his first night in freedom, that will be my first question, sort of a post-prison question, hardly onerous, and then we'll see what sort of answer he gives, perhaps all subsequent questions can be based on whatever he says, I have to provide him with elastic concepts, the main thing is that Tjaž comes out of himself, draws from his treasure chest, speaks from his inner reserves, mentions the turning points and diagonals, bridges the gulfs of memory and squirts as many facts as possible into my milk pail. But why limit myself to one night, why all this modesty, why not ask, as is only fitting, what season, century, what historical period Tjaž spent in the skyscraper café. I realize the answer will be difficult to produce, and I don't know if he'll be up to it, certainly this would have been long after the days of Cankar and Župančič. In as much time as Tjaž had spent up there, Cankar had already written seven plays, not that I would begrudge him that, who says so, but seven plays is still seven plays. Župančič, for his part, after such an interval, would already have been resting up after his first collection of poems, while Kette and Murn would have finished dying in the Ljubljana sugar mill, and throughout Carantania a passion for schisms, for insignificantly differing camps would have been born, even though all were faced with the same threat of annihilation, that didn't matter, they just kept splitting apart in their small-mindedness, a regular pettiness that took root, nickel and diming for the authority and dominance that would survive the destruction and come back with resurgent force post-extinction, a time of hair-splitters, therefore, that used phrases and traditions to split the body politic apart, they fed it so they could more easily split it apart, feed my sheep, so yes, Tjaž's trip to the skyscraper café belongs more or less to that era, as does my lurking at the foot of the café for him to return so I could slink him onto my tape, otherwise Tjaž's relationship to grazing and livestock was unspoiled, natural and pure up to this point, feed my sheep, not to mention the other livestock. Early on he had fulfilled all the preconditions of pasturage, he had driven more sheep out to pasture than he would have liked, had grazed sheep before school in spring, after school in autumn, instead of school in summer, grazing them at the side of county roads, near a stream, this side and that of the stream, in the stream and alongside it, in front of the stream and behind it, they'd grazed the stream, the road, and the hillsides, the county's ferns, and on the boundary between public and private sorrel he had grazed the sheep till he dropped. At that time Tjaž was still small, smallness was an inborn trait for him, from the start it had forced him to fend for himself, he tottered from one wet nurse to the next, crawled out of shorts and shirts one after the other, hung out in mud puddles and got in the way, grew as much as he could, at first he grew to the point he could manage a simple sheep pasture and acquiesce to their bleating. He wasn't able to prevent his father's birth, his father was born in a flash, amid the urgings of his parents, Tjaž's grandparents, he shot up as decisively as could be expected in that mountainous world and quite soon bade farewell to that lonely farmstead which could no longer feed them all, he set out on the best possible path for becoming Tjaž's father, he entered service, hired on as a hand for a well-to-do farmer and came to manage his land, he did a fine job handling the land and he also handled a girl, though she didn't need to be handled as carefully or as much as the land, so that father's handling of the girl only took place as the occasions arose, while handling the land required an employee's conscientiousness, even though the handling of the girl ploughed a far more fateful furrow than handling the land, because it was responsible for Tjaž coming down with both a father and a mother, he came down with them both in the same breath as the girl, out in some desolate part of the land, in some granaries, some huts, and some sheds, in the hay, straw, or moss came down with Tjaž, in the dark in one of the places just listed and one of the fodders just named father ignited a life for Tjaž in his mother's body, he became flesh and dwelled among us, came into the world, which at that time of course was no bigger than a pooped and peed-on diaper, and that's not much in the great, wide world. The hired hand and the girl had begun bed-ding each other without wedding each other, they gave it some time and hoped for time's curative power to come to their aid, but time didn't bother, they didn't particularly appeal to each other, so they bedded each other sluggishly, as much as they could stand, not much then, or that's what people, who always know everything, said, because there are no other sources, I depend on their gossip, the father himself was stubbornly tight-lipped about it and unavailable to this day, apparently he didn't think that far ahead, but when Tjaž happened to him there was no other choice but for the father and the mother to wed until they were dead. This is when the first green light shone into Tjaž's life, there were no obstacles remaining, Tjaž was able to start on his path. Soon after his arrival they moved off of the property so they could start their own household on a parcel of land that they leased and so father could get logging, each in his or her own way said good-bye to what they had laid claim to—the father to the meadows, fields, and fringes, to the livestock, the pastures, baskets, tree clefts, and harnesses, the tools, crops, and upland smells that the winds carried off into neighboring hollows, and the mother to her virginity, her succulence, and her youth. They wrapped Tjaž up in some rags and he lay on his back on the floor of the two-wheeled cart through the entire move, the orangeish trees and frayed clouds did nothing for him as the vehicle tossed and shook, the steel-hooped wheels revolving unevenly, bouncing, jolting, and lurching apart one instant, together the next, as it slid through thick and thin, first the right wheel would lag, then the left, and toward the end the path turned into a narrow sheep trail heading downhill with fences made of half timbers pressing in from both sides, and green straps of pastures behind them reaching for the path, till finally the wagon trail turned off into the woods. Several times little Tjaž tried to stick his hand in the spokes, but succeeded only once when they were already halfway there when the wagon tipped him on his side and he took advantage of the opportunity to stick his hand in the wheel, the spokes pecked angrily at his fingers and abraded the skin on his knuckles so that blood welled up. Tjaž bawled and held his bloody wounds up to view, hitting ever more

powerful registers, his father yanked wildly at the horse's reins, causing the jade to rear up on its hind legs, his mother came to the rescue, but Tjaž resisted with powerful kicks and scratches, he kicked
and scratched the furniture, clothes, and linen, the horse blanket,
the planks of the wagon, the reins—in short, everything he could
reach, this was the first time Tjaž's scratching instinct manifested
itself unambiguously, of course at that point the scratching was still
just a means, by no means an end, but it bore down with such fury
that nobody could have failed to notice Tjaž's gifts, which several
years later found ways to gather more and more support and at last
lay claim to broader and broader strata of fans until he got his first
open requests. From there to conscious, professional scratching
wasn't far, if we consider that no extra training was needed, the un-
teachable gift of scratching was always present, though invisible of
course to the ignorant and blind, who had no hope of figuring this
business out, much less expected to see something special grow out
of such modest beginnings. Indeed, several years later Tjaž got his
first official order in this line of work, it happened when he was
walking back to the institution as darkness was already shoving its
way between buildings, the streetlights greedily sucking it up, level
with a mechanic's repair shop there was a boy standing on the sidewalk, he had been waving to Tjaž from far off to follow him into the
courtyard. Soon Tjaž, suspecting nothing untoward, was standing
in the courtyard of the unlit repair shop, ready to offer his help or
at least satisfy his curiosity, why else would they have called for him
to come into the courtyard. The repair shop must have already
closed for the day, because there wasn't a living soul anywhere, not
a hint of workshop clatter, not a hint of the smell of gasoline, grease,
iron, and paint, the five or six iron doors were closed and locked,
just a few cars abandoned along the walls, waiting in vain to get
fixed today, nowhere was there a single light, nowhere the boy who
had waved from the sidewalk. It began to occur to Tjaž that something was wrong here, and he was just about to make a quick exit
when a bunch of boys rushed out from behind a car, surrounded
him in a trice, and blocked his path, the ring of boys' heads kept

getting denser as new ones joined from all sides, with four or five in each cluster, the ring quickly closed, he was trapped, but a scrap of hope flickered when he discovered a weak point in the ring, dashed in its direction, broke through, and set out at a sprint the length of the wall, past the cars, until the walls finally shut off his last way out, he didn't get far, trapped between the cars and the wall he had to admit there was no way out, he was trapped, and he anticipated nothing good coming from it, in a flash he'd correctly assessed his situation, that any further resistance would be risky and absurd, there was no more hope or chance of escape, Tjaž gave in to his fate and waited tensely to hear what would happen to him, things moved quickly from there, out of the ring came one boy's voice that sounded serious, even concerned, and Tjaž learned that the living ring consisted of boys from such and such boarding school, that they had heard about Tjaž's feats of scratching and had been eager to know more, from the very first mention, and today their trick had succeeded, they had kidnapped the scratcher with the intention of testing him, now it was Tjaž's turn to show them his skill by scratching up whatever they demanded, and it would be worth his while to cooperate with them, he wouldn't regret it if he would just oblige them without any delay and give them a chance to be present as he worked, watch from up close as he scratched, and with their own eyes determine how much bluff was involved, how much truth, what was the trick and how these skills could be further developed, what else they could be used for, and so on, in short, he was to show them right there how scratching was done, so they could judge its usefulness for their purposes. It did not escape Tjaž that, despite the reasonable words, there was a threat in the boy's voice, it was clear to him that the situation would not permit long discussions and speeches, action was needed if he was to get out of this vice, he understood that they hadn't caught him for fun or a joke, but with the intention of having him join them and scratch for them, he was expected to enter into their service. By nature he wasn't so tough that this sort of adventure didn't affect him, didn't leave him cold and impartial, subconsciously of course he didn't agree with the method by which they intended to win him to their side, or with the conditions under which he was supposed to display his scratching, but he realized that in such circumstances these things were of only peripheral importance, he had to reveal his art to these boys, he had to show them how he scratched, he had to introduce them to his craft, and he'd better not delay, because who knows who might wander into the courtyard and the delinquents would have to break up without achieving their aim. So Tjaž lost no time, he took aim at a truck that stood at the far end of the courtyard, he stabbed a nail into its windshield and started to turn it, he drilled a small hole through the pane until his finger was looking into the cabin, the eddies of his nails kept getting more brazen, the radius of the circle kept growing steadily, the nail drilled diligently and cut the pane into tiny bits, with glass slivers spraying in all directions like sparks from an axe being sharpened. When his nail hit the window frame, Tjaž stopped, the opening was so big now that it touched the metal frame on all sides and even the fattest boy could have stuck his head through. Little triangles of the pane still clung to the corners, Tjaž softly tapped on them with the pads of his fingertips, he gently touched the last remains before popping them out, the thick pane had worn out, it was gone, and now a hole gaped wide and the boys gaped back at the punctured truck, they hadn't had time to listen to Tjaž's nails or watch the process, barely had the glass first started to rattle when the work was suddenly done, they had missed their chance to observe him, hadn't registered Tjaž's gestures, grip, and stance, the details they'd wanted to note, it was as though they only woke up after it was all over, they perked up and approached, inspected the hole, because only now did they see it, they carefully felt around it, sniffed it, and touched it, it struck them dumb, took their breath away, at that moment they had forgotten about Tjaž, who could easily have run away from them if he had wanted, but there was no need, things had shifted to Tjaž's advantage, he began feeling victorious inside and it was clear that he was not only growing in their eyes, but that he had physically gained a fraction in height. From now on they would never again harass or trick him when they needed him, they would come for him in broad daylight and he would go scratch for them, melt some glass, undo some fabrics, saw some girls, loosen some wood, that was all, he helped them out when the need arose, and as time passed their collaboration cooled, but not before he had left a few more milestones behind. Tjaž's scratching services became domesticated and lost some of their glamour, they grew mundane, almost as imperceptibly mundane as they had been at one time, many years before, when Tjaž's family moved from hollow to hollow, that's when the little scratcher first tested his skills without his parents discovering them, perhaps the two-wheeled cart had transmitted some gift for scratching into his nails and sparked that ingenious notion in his mind, god knows, let's leave that to him, in any case Tjaž became aware of these qualities of his very soon, at the very least the household rummage that Tjaž had been trapped in for several hours straight was very conducive to his thinking more seriously about his fate, I can imagine that every jolt of the cart led to some new resolution. After the hitch left one hollow and before it turned into the next, they took a break, his father stopped the horse, tied the reins to a fence, and fastened a feedbag onto its head, alfalfa with a bit of straw, the horse started nibbling, a small stream stumbled past, the water ground away at the bank and slowly crept under the path, sand was slowly being ground out of the rock and some silt had bedded down next to the rushing water, the father and mother sat down at the side of the path so that Tjaž was within arm's reach, they took out some bread and sheep's cheese, offered a pat of cheese and a bit of bread to Tjažek with the intention of forestalling any new spree by his nails, but Tjaž cared for neither, I believe he launched the cheese first, then the bread, without racking his brain over the sequence beforehand, whether he should get rid of the bread first or the cheese, he had to start with something and of course it's possible that the bread was in line before the cheese, it just really doesn't matter, he made no such distinctions, paying no attention to the sequence he got rid of them both, he flung them away from himself with such force that they ought to have landed in the next hollow over, though in fact they fell into the grass alongside the path, far enough that they didn't fly back into the cart. That same evening the father and mother inaugurated their joint household in a cabin they'd leased with some grassland around it, the father began felling trees, the mother tending house, and Tjaž began accumulating his first little adventures, awkwardnesses, and bad luck, visits from the priest became more and more frequent until his parents were married in church, and after that the priest began to scale down his house calls, and Tjaž's parents came out ahead, all in all, because they had placed a foundation under their footsteps, equipped their life with a sturdy bottom, concluding a wedding allowed them to take part in the church's customs and folkways and become eligible for all of its goodies and treats, and in the end they would be allowed into heaven, Tjaž's presence had been legalized, all happiness awaited him, the marriage had been blessed, the house was safe from all evil, and a church burial was assured. But they didn't get far with their proper marriage, they'd started too late, the hitlerian war caught up with them and it became immediately clear that things wouldn't go well without his father, so his father set down his tools and picked up a weapon, he helped himself to all the war he could stand, gobbled it up till he dropped, but then hitler decided he wanted the mothers too, and fortunately there was still some room in the concentration camps, so he assigned Tjaž's mother to one of those, where she managed to nab a spare bunk, one of the last, at that time Tjaž was still totally useless, his nails' capacities still remained hidden, so he stayed at home like some sort of memento, somebody has to stay home, you can't just leave it empty. Among the first tasks awaiting him in the orphaned house was grandmother's death. It was never determined what she died from. At the time Tjaž was less than a novice at dying, all he remembers are the emissions from grandmother's lower body, which he took care of with white powder, he would shake powder onto the open, wrinkled skin three times, I think, if not more times per day, all in a row, morning, noon, and evening, at all the principal times when time would get thickest, but sometimes also when grandmother would begin to scream and then keep screaming until Tjaž shook white powder over her openings, only the white powder was able to quiet her down, and then grandmother would always stick a finger in the hole between her legs, which didn't keep Tjaž from continuing to shake powder from the cardboard box wherever the skin opened, then he would wait for the pus to absorb the powder before shaking out a new layer of powder, but gradually more and more and wider openings appeared in her skin and soon the powder stopped working and shaking it had no effect, the pus crept through the wrinkles into the sheets and mattress, and that's where grandmother somehow managed to die, she dried up the pus herself, gathered her courage one final time and slept some peace into her openings, she screamed sweetness and light and folkways and customs into them and died as dying was done in those days, the options were limited, there wasn't a very wide choice. A stranger traveling through later confirmed the time of grandmother's death on the basis of Tjaž's account in which there was a mighty boom in the kitchen and it suddenly occurred to him that the sideboard had tipped over and all of its porcelain and tin contents had crashed onto the floor with a terrible clatter, when in fact of course nothing like that had happened, that's what the stranger decided, and that's also what Tjažek convinced himself of, that the thunder had accompanied grandmother in her departure from this world and was an acoustic signal that Tjažek could stop powdering grandmother's openings once and for all. Soon after that they buried grandmother, there weren't many people, and practically no commotion, Tjažek felt a twinge in his chest, the funeral was terse, a few little prayers and quick signs of the cross and the shovels were already speaking and sealing the little mound of earth, they were in such a hurry that they chattered, and then the people hastily scattered. Then a far worse day dawned, stuffed full of hunger, cold, and corpses. Somehow Tjaž managed to get himself and the desolate leased property through all the horrors of those days, father came back bent and emaciated, the war looking out through his eyes, he and mother had ensured they would have a church burial, but mother no longer needed one, for she had burned up in the concentration camp's fire, now there was a little more room in the camps, and with father's return and mother's incineration the time of education started for Tjažek, and for the first time father hoisted his luggage in his once bearish hands onto his jutting shoulders and carried it to the station. Some rust-colored leaves lay in the station's vestibule, although there wasn't a single tree growing anywhere near the station, neither coniferous nor deciduous, nor any bushes, trees were forbidden, so where the leaves came from I don't know, the train kept repeating itself to the point of delirium, with acceleration after acceleration, chug after chug, stop after stop, wait after wait, they wandered the stations, inhaled the sooty smoke, and stared out through the windows at nature deformed until father and Tjaž finally stepped out on the city platform, father loaded Tjaž's suitcase up on his shoulder and they ploughed themselves a path through the crowd, some of whose shoulders collided with father all loaded down, but that didn't have any effect on him, neither good nor bad, while others intentionally slammed into him, so that he staggered and the luggage threatened to pitch until father caught his balance, but that didn't bother him either, walk behind me, he commanded, and on they went, walking wordlessly through the city, father in front, his son behind him, they walked through a good part of the city, rattled over a whole series of sidewalks, scurried past ruins and shell craters, the coarse peasant clothing rustled on father's limbs, Tjaž held close to father's heels, he was on father's heels, people turned around to look, first at them walking, one right after the other, then at the shouldered suitcase when everyone else carried them in hand, and finally at father's eccentric limp as he rustled along in his peasant suit, a log had once injured father's leg and although it had been fixed well enough for the country, it was no good anymore for the city, reason enough for people to turn and stare, while Tjaž walked empty-handed, bearing hard on father's heels, his body concealing father's limp from the people who turned to stare, but Tjaž was helpless against the people who came toward them, usually the ones in front and the ones behind were one and the same, because once they had noticed father's limp from the front they wanted to see it again from behind, and that's where Tjaž could conceal him with his little body, so that people barely saw half of father's limp, Tjaž gritted his teeth but still felt some satisfaction, better than nothing, there was nothing more he could do. And so they went, turning right and left, walking behind me, noticing the smooth walls straining the sunlight, until they were in front of the big maple door, until they discovered the institution, its dazzling sign attracting both pairs of eyes, the father read it and so did the son, it dawned on the father and on the son and on the holy spirit, as it was in the beginning, so now and forevermore, and also now, at every reading both heads moved from left to right, father had completed his task and now Tjažek would have to face his alone, so he set the suitcase down off his shoulder and limped out into the street, his head inclined forward, his arms and legs clumsily bowed, his body shifting into smaller and smaller heaps until the last heap, which was more like a dot, vanished, and when it vanished and there was nothing left on the street, Tjaž was still watching the dot that had been his father and had gone out into the distance, he felt a powerful draft pry his lips open, the taste of salt came gusting into his oral cavity, he pushed the maple door forward and it slowly gave way, he exhaled the cold air of the cabin and rang the bell, he became a boarding school student, got his own number, kept his number all those years, the institution entered his blood, made itself at home in his blood, and he started scratching, he gathered his first students around him, scratched his way through a whole series of tasks, de-shoed, peeled, tore, split, sliced, sawed, unscrewed, crushed, drilled, and de-glazed, he wanted a change of scene, tried things in freedom, at first he spent the night in the sky-scraper café, slept with a waitress by force of circumstances, perhaps just now had entered the elevator, pressed the button, and started down, he stands in the elevator, his feet planted wide, and he descends to the depths, through all the stories, piercing ceilings and floors, while at each floor the control panel clicks, it's a long way down, because the café is at the top of the tallest skyscraper in town, instead of a cross they put a café on top, it won't be long and the elevator will come to a stop, settling softly on the main floor, and from there on everything is clear, up to this point the conclusions are correct, the paragraphs in place, the chapters concluded, the pencils all sharpened, the story goes on, the bureau of reports will get its report on Tjaž on time, familiarize itself with it, have to take a position, say yes or no, one or the other or both, yesno or noyes, it sticks to its principles and doesn't deviate from them without good reason, we'll see, it's all the same to me, the tape recorder is on, the microphone is ready, the questions are on the tip of my tongue.

8.

A CHAPTER ABOUT
UNDRESSING

That morning when we were all assembled and waiting in the café for them to carry Tjaž in I will forget as soon as possible, at least I hope I do. I was on my way to school, I had just left the house when a messenger rushed up and all out of breath blurted the news at me that Tjaž had just committed suicide, that he had flung his body into the depths from the café terrace on top of the sky-scraper, that he had smashed into the sidewalk and then lay there lifeless. For a few moments I felt as if I had been doused with lead and that I would never again be able to free my sinews from its grip, perhaps even as if my heart had stopped beating for a few moments, it all happened so quickly that I simply wasn't up to it. So instead of shaking me, the news of Tjaž's death actually petrified me, it made me hard and stiff and welded my body and soul into a useless mass. If only I'd had just one moment to prepare, I would have regained my poise immediately and released that mass of body and soul, if, let's say, I could have seen the messenger coming or I could have pinched off just a tiny bit of time somewhere, the tiny bit that you need for a thought to crystallize into a decision, I would have con-trolled myself and asked coolly so what does that have to do with me, why don't you report that to the proper authorities and so on, if only I could have, I would have concealed it without any regrets, as would only be fitting for a boarding school student, I would have acted on the principles that we have been educated in for years, the nuns could have been proud of me and probably would have point-ed to me as an example for all the other girls. So it's no doing of mine that I veered out of the furrow that had been ploughed for us and acted on my own, I didn't do it out of conviction, nor was it the result of any virtue, I did it out of confusion, a shortage of time, the news reached me unprepared and ill-disposed, I didn't even suspect, I was still holding onto the door handle or maybe had just let it go, I don't recall, in my mouth there were still the last bites of bread that there was no time left to eat in the room, because I was late as usual and generally swallowed the last bits of bread while I ran down the stairs or even outside, circumstances conspired against me, at the most inappropriate moment the messenger ran into me with his news in such haste that it knocked me flat and the real person couldn't help but leap out of me, the person I was in reality, naked and natural, endowed with senses and instincts, elemental and alive, and not the one I'd been educated to be and consequently even presumed that I was and suffered greatly when I couldn't be. Although Tjaž's demise wasn't a suitable occasion for this, still it made me experience myself again, after so much barren time this experience of my own self was so moving and did body and soul so much good, I sensed that I knew how to be good, I realized that I am good when I'm natural, that I'm beautiful when I'm naked, which is to say free of all educational appendages and societal rubbish, that I'm strong when I faint from weakness, and that I act truly when I act instinctively. So, like a wounded animal I dashed after the messenger, who didn't wait for an answer, he had knocked me flat and then left me alone, left me in the lurch, I ran after him the whole way without being able to catch up with him, and I remember perfectly the bite of bread that was still in my mouth from breakfast and that I should have swallowed but couldn't because my jaw wouldn't obey me, my teeth resisted, my saliva hardened and turned into lumps, at first tiny, then bigger and bigger, real lumps that started rolling around in my mouth, I kept trying to crush them with my tongue, chew them and push them against the roof of my mouth, back and forth, up and down, back and forth, up and down, I tried to spit the mass of them out, but my tongue got stuck, it wouldn't work, it refused to shove the blob out, and in the meantime the lumps kept growing and covering every last nook and cranny of my mouth, I couldn't close my mouth no matter how hard I tried. And so we ran and eventually arrived at the foot of the skyscraper and I saw that some men were measuring its height from the sidewalk up to the top of the skyscraper, from the top of the skyscraper down to the sidewalk, their eyes running from bottom to top and from top to bottom, from right to left and from left to right, from the side to the center and from there like rays of light out to all sides, it was clear they were measuring very precisely and consciously, and finally when they had taken all of its measurements, jotted them down, memorized them, and drawn lines across and diagonally and every which way, when they had unfolded a network of white lines in the courtyard, we carefully stepped over it, entered the elevator, and, leaning on the wall, inhaled clouds of breath, his breath had stunk of garlic or hot peppers, the stench filled the cabin up to the ceiling so that we couldn't talk, as the floors and staircases swooped past us. The café was stuffed full of frightened, whispering people running this way and that, although they didn't have a reason to be frightened, whispering and running, because Tjaž's death couldn't affect them, and it wasn't as though they gave a damn—instead, they were all those things because they happened to have some time to spare and so they were going to use it for something useful, and death is always useful, the death of a stranger is always welcome, they don't begrudge him his death because it tickles them and pleasantly stimulates their self-preservation hormones. As we pushed our way through the crowd, it rustled, the heads stretched and the necks stretched, and if there happened to be the first signs, just the tip of some intuition in their movements, the intuition turned into a hunch and the hunch was transformed into indignant certainty accusing me of the basest contact with Tjaž, and that tip locked me into a causal relationship with his death, even though it's unlikely that any of them had ever seen me in his company. Each of us waited in his or her own way and for something else, I was waiting for the men who were going to carry Tjaž up to the top, and the crowd was waiting to see how I would behave, we all concealed our feelings, but everyone knew about them and it wouldn't have made any difference if we didn't conceal them. If there had been more room in my heart for hatred, I would have hated all of them right down the line, I would have scratched their eyes out and shoved their pig snouts in their own shit, but my breast had drunk its fill of pain and fear, it was overthreatened and overexposed, uncertainty had deformed it and deprived it of all decisiveness, it felt outwitted, betrayed, and deceived, it couldn't find any sense in all of this, and I fled deep into myself, where I cowered in the quietest corner. We waited, and the longer we waited, the more the waiting turned into lurking, that was the true essence of waiting, we were each of us on the lurk for our prey, and from somewhere farther on a commotion announced itself in the stairway, so they're already on the way here with him, they're carrying him, I'd never seen a corpse or an injured person being carried, but I knew that they would carry him in one very particular way if he was dead, and a different way if he was alive, there was something inside me that said they were going to carry him in on their shoulders, dead, that he would be floating over the heads of his bearers, but just over the floor if he was alive, they would hold him just far enough up off the floor, a little higher in the back than in the front, in any case just off the floor. My next logical assumptions led me to the thought that if he was dead, the stretcher would be heavy and would bear down with all its weight toward the floor, so that the men would have to hoist him onto their shoulders, while if he was alive, then the strength of their arm muscles would suffice, because the stretcher would dangle cheerfully in their hands, they would walk upright and proud, as though they had protected him, had saved his life. So if they carry him in on their shoulders, he's dead, and if he's dangling down near the floor, he's alive. I weighed these two possibilities the entire time we waited for them to carry him in and we first heard the noise from below, listened to their footsteps slowly approaching, which eventually turned into clatter and stumbling and sometimes got lost in some wall, and I realized that one of these two possibilities had long since been realized, that he was either dead or alive, there was no other possibility, and that my speculations were nothing more than guessing about a completed and concluded event, and today I'm amazed that that weighing of mine could raise any doubts, if I think about the height, the concrete sidewalk, and Tjaž's frail, unhardened body. The gasping for breath kept getting closer, the stairs were wearing the carriers out, the stretcher must have been of some great if indeterminate weight, if I give it serious thought, the burden got in the way of their walking, it wasn't footsteps I heard, but slipping and stumbling, clearly the building wasn't built for carrying corpses, each time the bearers bumped into a wall, collided with a door frame, smashed some plaster, swore and gave orders, or shifted the stretcher into every possible position as they turned a corner so they could slink around it while making sure the one they were carrying didn't slip off, the noise of it echoed distinctly. Tjaž's death wasn't meant for that building or for those people, he should have died at some other time and in some other place, in late autumn or winter, for instance, when people are tired from the summer or from collecting the fruits of autumn, but he never had much luck at choosing, least of all that last time, he was short on imagination. He would go to bed, wake up, go back to bed, and in between there was all that superficial circus clowning around which really should have offered him countless opportunities for making his decision—the one last choice that a person has in this world—so I just can't believe that these opportunities were all absent for Tjaž, it just doesn't make sense to me that he didn't do better for himself. Take, for instance, death in the bathtub. Why couldn't he have chosen that, the time Saturday afternoon or even evening, the place the bathtub at home, you've noisily lumbered your way through the streets, the hallways and offices, attended to your tasks from dawn to dusk, and this time, let's say, you're tired and depressed, the work you've done didn't exactly give you a boost, didn't move you forward, or only just far enough for you to hold steady and not slip behind, you've had a bad day, you've always done half-hearted work, and today perhaps just half of the usual half-heartedness, and now you submerge your body in the water and listen to it soothing your limbs, all over your body you feel healing caresses, the bath removes the weight of the day you've now completed, you spread soap over your skin, splash the water so that it foams, you bathe full steam ahead and in the true sense of the word, you wash yourself intently, yet at the same time very carefully, so as not to wash off that thin film that your last prohibited lover imprinted on you during your lunch break, you try very carefully not to scrub off her scent, which your body has taken on, you bathe a long time until you feel that you're clean, but it wasn't cleanliness you bathed for, that's just a pretense for bathing, your thoughts grow dull and you have no taste for plans for tomorrow or the day after, you don't feel up to them, you've done enough today and now you're finished, you drive off all strenuous thoughts, tomorrow is Sunday, you won't get up before ten, it's the only day when you can sleep in, before you get out of the bathtub you'll run a cold shower over your back, a habit you've kept from your boarding school days, but this thought is unpleasant so you put it aside, the water soothes you, you dream with the tips of your fingers, you sink into the water up to your ears, the water reaches up to your mouth, you can see that this is the time, you're locked in and there's nobody near, your death would slip past people almost imperceptibly, only your immediate surroundings would learn of it and you would hardly notice it yourself, you'd have a beautiful death, a lot of people would envy you for it, and now you're probably sorry that you let so many perfect opportunities go by, but it's too late, you had to be difficult. All indications are that the bearers have appeared at the top of the steps with their cargo, the first thing we saw was the sheet covering something, then the stretcher, and only then the heads and shoulders, so they'd carried him in on their shoulders, as I'd been privately hoping all along, I wouldn't have been up to the occasion if it had been any different, I wouldn't have known how to greet him if he'd come in in some other way, I couldn't have stood the look of his eyes, I wouldn't have known how to answer his moans, even if I'd understood them, it's best this way, I had hoped he would be dead, and now it was true, he really made that moment easy for me—I say easy, because the entire time we knew each other he was understanding and considerate of me, there was no one more socially sensitive than him, I really feel sorry for him, but there's nothing I can do, the memory of him will remain pure and unsullied, I admire the consistency of his thinking, even though his final step seems inconsistent to me, or at least not in accordance with his convictions, but he undoubtedly had his reasons, though I probably wouldn't say that if I knew what they were, I can't say anything against him even though I'd like to, I'd have to invent something, in fact there's nothing left for me here, I saw them carry him in on their shoulders and look for a place to set him down, and with that my work is done, I could have slipped out through a crack in the crowd, but even so I held out for a while longer, I wasn't feeling particularly well. The procession had since moved into the café and it was like in a church, the men set their load down, people crowded around the stretcher, and when they pulled the sheet off, or perhaps they didn't actually pull it off but just thought about pulling it off, I closed my eyes. I had to close them tight and very forcefully, with a bang so to speak, or to put it in other words, I slammed them shut so it hurt and the pressure of my eyelids triggered a pleasant solitude in me, I couldn't explain to myself where this incredible, solitary, unearned peacefulness came from, this pleasant, delightful repose, this ease like a rainbow butterfly. At first I could still make out the roofs of individual buildings, but then, when they began to spin around my head, leaving a narrower and narrower ring of sky up above, then merged into a long, gray wall that stretched out wide with no end in sight, I was on a merry-go-round and then off it again, because I felt as though a vortex of hot sand was sucking me in and forcing my breath out, then suddenly wasn't sucking me in because I felt as though I'd been wound up into a little ball and was slithering horizontally backward, that my heart and lungs were pressing against the ice-coated wall of my throat, that my spine was being completely unscrewed, and that my body was bulging, turning into a larger and larger balloon that was going to take off into the wind any second, then the balloon image vanished, because I was speeding downward past walls instead of up with the wind, constantly downward, floor after floor went darting past me, the falling became unbearable, the skyscraper was deep, monstrously deeper than it was high, the streets had no floor and the sidewalk no bottom, the network of white circles and lines grew into a hiding place, a fragile landing spot, a detestable mortuary, a vertiginous chessboard, and on this huge chessboard, on a mysteriously black square, a wild horse was waiting that was going to shove me into a corner with its hoofs, if there was anything left from the fall to shove, and keep me in check, if there was anything left from the fall to keep in check, so that I couldn't move, I fly toward it, although I was just at the top of the skyscraper and just squeezed my eyes shut harder than I meant to when they brought Tjaž in on their shoulders, I shut my eyes and triggered the spinning, and now I'm plummeting into the bottomless depths, and there's no question that I'm going to crash into an anvil any instant and fly apart, or that my body will be splattered all over the ground. I've already winced, the better to endure that last stab of pain, but when I opened my eyes, I was still flying past buildings toward the courtyard, there was still no end, there is still no end, there won't be an end, and instead of approaching, the courtyard was now receding and I couldn't tell anymore whether I was racing down or up, in or out. Far down below the chess horse had slipped its hitch, it was gone, the courtyard was empty. When I smashed into the ground, my body stretched out, my face dug into the soft dirt up to the ears, kneeling, my hands pressing against the ground, I pulled my face out of the earth with soft dirt still clinging to it, my temples throbbing painfully. I had barely brushed the film away from my eyes and opened them when I found myself lying in my former bed at the boarding school, and that was the strangest and most incomprehensible part. Am I conscious or not, and where am I, I felt that just then, as I was just coming to, unless I was only then fainting away, everything preceding that had just been a joke, but this was the beginning of my real state of unconsciousness, doubts pounced on me left and right, what is actual reality and what only seems real, what is unconsciousness and what is consciousness, my eyes widened and I must have been staring more than insanely into space. I was overcome with gratitude, because the spinning had turned out all right against all expectation and hadn't ended on the sidewalk as Tjaž's had. I was grateful, even though I didn't know who to be grateful to, but at the same time I was overcome with horror at the latest events in the café, which announced themselves to my memory with perfect clarity and were proof that I must have been conscious, after all, I wasted a lot of time trying to figure out how I'd gotten to the boarding school when I didn't live there anymore, how I'd managed to navigate into my former bed, wake up amid the old furniture, the vase of flowers on the table, the white window, the view of the chapel, everything as it had been. In fact this was no longer my bed, my vase or my window, even though they had once been mine, but not any longer, so much had changed since the time when I had to leave the boarding school. The familiar boarding school smell assaulted my nostrils, and I stared at those unfamiliarly familiar walls and couldn't get enough of them, I was in the old house, had scooped it up once again with my senses, but it wasn't it I inhaled, it was Tjaž, I inhaled him as freshly as I had at one time in these rooms, and now, when I was back in my old home, he approached me again and stopped at a distance, that must have been outside these walls, out near the chapel, rather far from here, so I reached out toward him who was no longer reachable from my level, although he was present, each of us stood at his post, I couldn't reach him anymore, and the more I tried to approach him to trade glances and capture just one shared glimmer, the more he retreated, the more the walls shoved in between us, the more the chapel came to light. I stopped summoning him from the background, the pain got stuck in my flesh, my flesh shuddered and throbbed several times and then chafed, and I know that it's over, at least it was over, and if it was no longer possible to redeem myself, I couldn't fend off the tears, they crept into the twisted furrows on my face, the furrows channeled them, and they flowed down the channels to my ears and from there they dropped into my blanket, so I must have loved him too, I recall that I didn't cry from any need of my own, but due to external factors, so it's true what he said, that we had accumulated too much of each other, become too dense with each other and too intimately absorbed one another, now they were setting him down on the stage up in the café, that's far from here, yes, it's far from here, it has to be far from here, it always was far from here, there's nothing transitory about his body, he hasn't changed the way funeral biers change people, he'd just come back from a party with a song on his lips and bright color in his eyes, the remains of a dance in his joints and with fidgety hands, with a crisp skin which could also have been—let's get it said—the skin of an ash or a maple. Then, when that thing with Tjaž happened, I was in the second form, and soon after that the nuns threw me out of the boarding school, I rented a room in town, and that thing happened far away from the nuns, in the sense of both time and space, at a time, then, when I was rooming alone under the roof of a four-story building. This was the first time in my life that something happened away from the nuns, so to speak, but it soon turned out that it hadn't happened without their involvement, because hardly had news spread of Tjaž's unhappy demise, which shook me unconscious—or, let's put it this way—hardly had I blinked, reflexively, the better to withstand the blow and build my strength back up in my sleep, so in other words even before everything was over and Tjaž had found his rest, than I was suddenly back in their hands, it was never too late for them, they tore me out of one environment and planted me in another, paying no heed to my feelings and my emotional state, so throughout the time I was rooming they were firmly behind me, right on my heels they were waiting for the moment to pounce, to drag me out of the muck and drive me out of my home, but they didn't let me out of their sight, I had apparently left them some hope, otherwise they wouldn't have taken the initiative with me that they did. If the mere thought of their institution revolted me even before that, the realization that in the bitterest, most trying moment of my life I had woken up there once again took all the life out of me. In that state the nuns revealed yet another surprise to me, namely that everything that had gone before would be forgotten, because one needed to draw a line under one's sinful past and start anew, and that now I could make a new start, right away, live in their school once again, since my departure no one had taken my place, even though they could have, because they were sure I would come back contrite as I had now in fact done, that they had prayed for this day to come, and so on. I don't know where I found the strength to refuse, to thank them for their charity and compassion, but explain that it had come at an extremely unfortunate time for me, what was I supposed to do with it at this hour, I had long since given up passing my afternoons and evenings with cloistered pieties, which perhaps just that morning had rung their last, but till then had been ringing pretty much constantly, the way emptiness rings when you run into it, or even just touch it, or when the wind drives trash into it. Hollow experiences crush you, you try shaking them off without being able to get rid of them, you long for abundance because you've never tried it, you hold out your dish, and the longer you hold it out, the less selective you become, your suffering runs out, you're happy with anything, you see, that's when Tjaž appeared and promised me change and a rest, and because I was young and pretty, he also promised me heaven, as we say, I have to confess that he took his promise very seriously and conscientiously, even though he couldn't carry it out, but that's not his fault, he was already carrying inside him that word of his that ultimately shoved him to his death, if my suspicions are correct, that secret, concealed word—always unspoken, but always ready to be spoken if only the right opportunity arose, or perhaps even just the opportunity of an opportunity would have sufficed—that hovering, explosive word, which at the slightest touch would have ignited, that smoldering, surging word buried in butts and ashes, that forbidden, unwanted word that was all of these things at once and each of them separately, that suppressed and downtrodden word, that's what Tjaž carried inside him, deep in his wanting, in each separate red blood cell and each separate white blood cell, in every fiber of his being, which is finished now, in every granule of breath, carefully guarded and secretly tended, fearfully uneasy—and "fearfully" isn't just a turn of phrase—never at rest, always primed and ready, that violent, corrosive, murderous word. One day when by chance we caught sight of, ran into each other outside, each of us walking on our side of the street with the chestnut trees in between, I sensed that he intended it for me. He gave himself some more time for reflection and ripening, in other words he held off till some other day, and in fact the nicest part of all was waiting for what I knew would soon have to happen, and a few days later it actually did happen, he stopped me and pronounced his word, which had been longing to be pronounced as soon as possible, he waited for me outside the second form's building, and there he confessed to me, something he probably never before had a chance to do, I doubt he had ever before experienced love, affection, and warmth, perhaps he didn't search for those things enough and just wished for them, just dreamed and longed for them with his arms crossed, waited indolently for them, instead of taking decisive action, and in fact even in my case he only did that later, after I approached him. In spite of everything I dwelled only on the appearance of his word, I only perceived the sound and color of his voice, I failed to pick up on its inner tension, and today I realize that I didn't properly comprehend the anxiety that clung to each syllable, I didn't re-experience the great and simple truth that made his word great and simple, and I also think that I didn't reckon with the possibility that the word could be born of torment and sorrow, just the opposite, I made believe and pretended I didn't hear it, and finally I consented, since because of the emptiness I was open to anything and at least it promised some change. We met twice a week on Tjaž's free afternoons, then he started coming to visit me in the evenings and I didn't deny him that either, though I was fully aware of the severity of the transgression. Our acquaintance still remained hidden from the nuns, later we began risking more and more, he experienced his first orgasms with me, he would stay until morning and now that he's dead I can say it, I let him because it suited me, for fun and out of curiosity, I helped him to get all the things he'd wasted and missed under his belt, at first he would leave very depressed and worried,

his conscience stung him and he was alive with remorse, at the
thought of the boarding school he would be seized by an animal
anxiety, but gradually he adapted, I calmed him down, explained
things to him and persuaded him, and together we tamed the fits
and the visions and things were all right, something inside him split
in two and something else turned around, I could feel it turning
around and taking new shape inside him, it was like something with
yeast was rising inside him, he loved me out of rebellion, deliberately, and out of spite, and in me he found a way of getting out of
his rut, he never treated me badly, he didn't have a drop of meanness
in him, I have to admit that and if he were still alive I would still
admit it, I'm not talking about him this way just because he's dead,
he was good to me, and as proof let me mention that he bought me
a watch, a pendant, books, and other things that I needed or wanted, even though he was penniless, he knew how to guess that stuff,
he was always gentle and considerate, and the only thing that humiliated me about the whole business was the feeling that he saw
me more as a means than a goal, and maybe I only imagined this,
but I feel vindicated by the fact that we didn't have anything serious
in mind, and ultimately it didn't bother me at all, I made peace with
it, but I didn't do it for nothing, I saw to it that I wasn't deprived,
he wasn't the first or the last man, he was one of those who are just
born different, are unique and therefore somehow the first and the
last all at once, what I mean to say is that this young man realized
himself with my help, he became Tjaž as he never was before me
and never was after me, the most real, authentic, and original Tjaž
that there ever was, unmatched by anyone, I'm convinced, anywhere
in the world, otherwise unmatched by anyone at any time and for
any reason and in any respect and in any print run, and I doubt—to
repeat my assumption—that this peculiar person had ever truly dug
through his nature before and turned up all his emotional and physical virtues and applied them to any great passion, and even if he did
turn them up, who would he have shown them to, he considered all
of that too great an indecency and a sin, he would rather have re-
nounced them and repressed them by force, Tjaž was no hero, he

lacked the courage and confidence, he was afraid that the passion of lovemaking would burn him up, for example, that amid the exertion and excitement he would drop dead, be snuffed out like a candle, that it would pierce him right through, perhaps sting him during the first quarter of the cycle, meaning he probably wouldn't even make it to the finish, end of story, death tying him up once and for all at precisely the moment when his orgasm began, so that he wouldn't be around anymore for its end, he was always nervous and terrified about the possibility of that happening, although it would have been an easy and beautiful end, it would have been a downright delightful, fairy-tale death, but no, Tjaž was by no means a hero, at the most he was a hero at the moment when he decided to jump off the tallest skyscraper in the whole city, but that was later and during his final moments, and then just enough for him to acquire a heroic reputation right before his end, hero or not, let him be whatever he wanted. As far as our time together was concerned, I have to note that he lacked resolve, if you will, in making decisions, that casts a bit of a pall on his character, I remember for example that I offered him an opportunity very early on, but he kept delaying and delaying, he just couldn't make up his mind and he only relented when we identified a whole series of shared paths and points of departure in our lives, and today it's clear that all that was just blind, empty coincidence, but at the time we ascribed great significance to it, we determined that we had been made for each other, how shallow and silly, back then even I believed in such silliness, all the signs pointed, or at least we pointed them toward the fact that we were meant for each other and that with the accretion of these shared and similar fortunes we could allow ourselves some proper passion. And so it came about that all the barriers between us began to collapse, it happened very quickly, they collapsed all at once and at the same time, or to put it directly, we went all the way. It was my fault that we broke up, I admit, I gave him back everything I had received from him, I wanted to hurt him and make him want to leave me, I had grown tired of him, I couldn't deal with his dullness and his darkness any longer, but I had no idea and no in-

tention that he would end up so miserably, none of it has anything
to do with his suicide, he never talked about suicide and he never
once hinted at it, even his behavior would never have led one to
such a conclusion. The evening before his death he deglazed my
window and scratched out the lightbulbs, you know about that
business, but how am I supposed to have reacted and how am I supposed to have correctly understood this as a cry for help, I came to
other conclusions, he never could stand glass, everything made of
glass revolted him and he would attack it wherever he had the
chance, he hated all glass things, it must have been something left
over from his earliest years, some bit of unfermented childhood
connected to glass or something like that, what do I know, he never
talked about it, I can imagine a bullet fired through a window, a
bomb or grenade fragment, shattered panes and windows patched
over with cardboard, glass shattering at some horrifying event, in
any case something that draped fear on the wall of his heart for all
time, some complex that clearly burdened him and caused him to
hate and that he tried to assuage by glazing things over on the one
hand and deglazing them on the other. I still vividly remember the
day when, out of the blue, without any reason, after a glass had
dropped to the floor and shattered, he revealed his gift for scratching to me, the first victims who had incurred the first scratches, but
you know all about that, I couldn't believe the beginning, that sort
of behavior struck me as childish and senseless, later I accompanied
him several times on his scratching expeditions and enjoyed them
more than I can say, there were some things that he scratched to
pieces just for my benefit, the scratching would lash out of him and
he would come to life in a way that I never saw otherwise, and ever
since then I thought differently of him, he didn't do it just for a lark,
it was serious business for him, because the scratching completed
him, he used it to shape his life, to hold his fate in balance, to perfect his personality, in short, without the scratching he wouldn't
have been able to live, and living means being free, deciding between options, enduring, being now and later, being always, and
then even after. Now he's dead and lying in the café, he's scratched

his way to his last target, a disfigured creature of skin and bones, a rubber-eyed, plastic-limbed person, smudged spittle, in his half-opened mouth the scream still visible but frozen, he must have passed out halfway down, it hardened in him before he had a chance to produce any sort of sound, a short, sharp scream like the ones frogs emit before a scythe cuts them in two, you can see he must have died with that scream in his mouth and now he lies here, you can see the jump from a great height in him, and though only he is at fault, he accuses us of ugly behavior, which is out of place, he killed himself, that's been proven and will yet be proven, we didn't kill him, our conscience is clear, but still he doesn't let up, he keeps pointing his finger at us, now that he's dead, especially now, he hides under a black veil, but he points it at us, of that you'll have no doubt in the coming few days, he's aiming at me, at you, at him, at her, at it, I'm aiming, you're aiming, he, she, and it are aiming, we're aiming, all of you are aiming, they're aiming, just as I'm aiming at you, you at him, he at her, she at it, it at the two of us, the two of us at the two of you, the two of you at the two of them, the two of them at all of us, we at you, you at them, they at me, everyone is pointing, nobody's not pointing, it's the same thing, he's lying dead in the café and even so, he still finds time and a way and a shape to point at a person, there are people around him, a crowd of people jostling around his coffin, offering me their hands, one after the other, in the room, on the stairs, in the auditorium, at the station, outside the door, in the courtyard, everywhere they're shaking my hand, there's more sorrow than a person can swallow, as much sympathy as you can bear, as much compassion as you can withstand, but it doesn't escape me that their gestures all hint at some superficial impression, the proper mournful pose, the sobbingly uttered word, they've practiced this at home and now they've got the hang of it, their sorrow suits them well, but in their hearts they rejoice at having got yet another new person onto the funeral bier. There he lies now and the people keep coming, some for coffee, others for a bite to eat, still others for beer or mineral water, and others yet again for the waitress—yet all of them in passing for Tjaž, it doesn't cost anything, it's never cost anything. Tjaž always came cheap, he never knew how to hold up his price or drive it even higher. The sun colors their profiles against the wall, longish heads appear, narrow shoulders, hollow chests, animalish backs, the teeth of mad dogs, scarecrows, bumpkins, gargoyles, masks. I'm not in the café, I think, because I came to at the girl's boarding school, let's say instead at my old home. The time will come for us to bury Tjaž and forget him, he doesn't deserve to have us remember him, it will be enough if only I remember him, on behalf, so to speak, of everyone else and at the request of all the others who don't like that sort of thing, and there are a lot like that, but Tjaž has himself to blame, he was my personal cause and, since he's been dead, my personal property, part of my real estate, if I can put it that way, part of my furniture, nothing more than a table or wall hanging, I'll have to do something with him, but I'm not yet sure just what, he can't stay there forever or even temporarily, he and I will have to move somewhere. When the nuns found the two of us out, they threw me out of the boarding school, because there was no alternative, that's when we moved into the attic room, that was our refuge, that's where we continued and kept going, where can we move now and how are we supposed to keep going, god only knows, they'll throw him out onto the street at the very least, if not into the gutter or onto some dung heap, a bonfire, or maybe into a wolftrap, that's obvious, they're not going to tolerate him for long in the café, a café is a café and not a morgue or a furniture warehouse, we're going to have to do something, except that I don't yet know just what, a girl feels an uncertain, inevitable task like this most acutely of all. Whenever I lie down at night and examine my body in the mirror, I notice that something's missing, something's not right with it, and lately I've figured out that my body misses Tjaž, it had gotten used to him, he was so gentle and considerate with it and if I said not today, then he would do nothing, that's how he was, but I always said yes, because it gave me pleasure, I've already told you about that, how he covered every tiniest part of my body with his lips, kissed every tiniest fiber of my skin, covering every part systematically and in sequence, from the front and the back, from the bottom and the top as well as from the sides, I felt as though he were covering all of me, softening me up on the inside and melting me on the outside, damming up the waves of my blood, like a tree in spring my sap started to run thanks to him, of course I contributed to his also coming and falling peacefully to sleep, I couldn't complain, it's a shame, all that is gone now, I don't understand how he could take his own life, I let him do whatever he needed, I'm not aware of ever not satisfying him or not meeting his needs, so I'm not to blame, he came and went of his own accord, I never forced him to go anywhere or lured him away from anyplace, his hands were free, he had free will, he came and went as he saw fit. I don't demand any more than that for myself, equal rights for both, I'm still young and I'll find another man, you must understand, I gave Tjaž his due, so with a clear conscience I can put aside everything that reminds me of him, I've only spoken about him because I thought I might be able to contribute some representative details to help clear up this unpleasant incident. Before I shut up about Tjaž and put the whole business behind me once and for all, before I conclude, therefore, I would also like to add a request that you not take my statement as some mere formal addendum, an attempt to tie up loose ends, so to speak, just because protocol requires a second and third point of view, quite the opposite, you need reliable, original contributions and credible sources, and if I've spoken about Tjaž now, then this has been the narrative of an eyewitness and a fellow participant, while simultaneously being a victim's statement, all this information was a part of Tjaž's essence, I lay claim to the admission that I more than knew Tjaž, that I could see deep inside his soul—even though we were close for only a short period of time—and that in said short time I helped shape his life, I even flatter myself that I saw through him more quickly and grasped him more deeply than all those people who spent years and decades with him, I'm not ashamed of my relationship to him, I know what you think and I know all about your sanctimonious insinuations, everything that you've imagined and suggested—well, we actually did it, every bit of it, and did it consciously, often and regularly, and I see no reason for me to leave those things out, so now you know about that too, so you can be open with me and call each thing by its real and, preferably, the first name that comes to your lips, I don't like deception, authenticity is what I got from him, who was extremely direct about what he wanted. I wouldn't have to testify about this if I didn't want to, of my own free will, the nuns did their best to shield me from it, they spirited me off to safety first thing, pleaded with the higher authorities on my behalf, and got them to forego a statement from me, they wouldn't have needed me if I myself hadn't seen to it that they did, my contribution wasn't important to them, they would have overlooked me without hesitation as they went sniffing through his past, but then I would have had to keep silent about the person who lives inside me, even now that it's all over. I didn't always think and feel the way I think and feel now, it's only now that I think and feel this way, and that's his doing, I have to chalk that up to him, he ploughed me up without my ever being aware of how or when, but he ploughed me up nevertheless and now I'm no longer the same person I was before, and I'll let it keep sprouting inside of me, that's a fine resolution, so now let me finish. I'm going to protect the life that was begun in me at this hour until it buds, and that's one more reason I didn't comply with the nuns' wishes, even though they had never before interceded on my behalf as vigorously and determinedly as then, but unfortunately one vigorous fart doesn't erase all the rest of the old-maidish behavior they subjected me to, and as you've seen for yourselves, I came here on my own initiative and of my own free will and against the will of my former guardians to speak from my own experience about Tjaž.

9.

A CHAPTER ABOUT
WILD BOARS

Although we don't have much to do with this business, Tjaž's tragic death was a blow to us, there can be no doubt about that, since he was among us for a quite a while and had grown close to our heart, as they say, we registered his death, which was for the most part an obvious business, and we noted it accordingly, but it created no particular work for us, and given how very busy we are that's quite important, because Tjaž had already left the institution and we had already taken care of all those things and taken all the steps of an administrative nature that are necessary at the departure of a student from the boarding school, to be candid, basically unpleasant things, and if we hadn't already taken those steps, we would have to take them now, and the difference wouldn't just be one of time, it would also be a lot more unpleasant now, but as it is all that is behind us now thank god and we have a bit more time and space for the essential things that particularly have to do with Tjaž's tragicomic actions and more generally with his tragicomic views. The school administrator has deleted him from all the registers and lists and god knows that didn't involve much, so the necessary entries were soon deleted and next year somebody else will be able to occupy his spaces, get his number, take his seat, fill in the gap in our numerical sequence, and so balance our statistics, which were slightly disrupted by Tjaž's departure, but that's no reproach, just a statement of fact, because the demand for space in boarding schools is enormous, so there's no risk that Tjaž's place will go unoccupied. The laundry was also assigned to collect and bundle up any of his clothes still in the tubs and cauldrons and send them after him, preferably to his home address, likewise there were a few items of clothing left lying in the seamstress's workroom, essentially worthless, and finally we checked in the cellar without being able to find anything of his, though, as I've said, all of that was irrelevant now, everything had already been prepared and, as it seemed, planned, so all that remained to be done was to register his death, to nod, so to speak, to acknowledge it with a nod, dot the *i*s, and that's what we did, in great Christian sorrow of course, and in keeping with all the rules of the most sincere compassion and good breeding. Not much data has been gathered about Tjaž, only the most important, and ours is probably the only place that collected vital data about him, it's scarcely worth mentioning, but some material did get collected, both good and not particularly good. There's no doubt that he made an effort, we cannot conceal or deny him a share of good will, absolutely not, that would not be Christian and, now that he's dead, it would be absolutely inappropriate, because whatever we tried had to be based on Christian principles, and whatever was based on Christian principles we tried, it couldn't be otherwise, that's what every community requires, but on the other hand he didn't make a sufficiently determined and forceful effort, so that the bad aspects often predominated, sadly that can happen, it has in the past and it will in the future, god help us. Tjaž's path led uphill and it was simply steeper and more stressful than others, he walked it with the intention of walking it to the end, that's what we think, and the institution did its very best to help him along, we gave to him, and he took, which is only fair, that's how it should be, we deliberately did not expect any other kind of relationship and there would have been no need, because each individual has to fight for these in his own way, take free will for instance, the fundamentals of our training are so simple and easy to grasp, they left countless opportunities for personal discovery and freedom, it's just that god didn't give Tjaž the ability to hear or see those delicate shades of his grace, it can hardly be a coincidence that of all our students he was the only one to end that way, just him and nobody else, as if by plan, that fact should give any doubter pause. Those of us who more than knew Tjaž, who saw into the depths of his soul, even though we were close only briefly, those of us who in that short time helped shape his life—that group of us even fancies that we saw through him faster and understood him more profoundly than all those who were together with him since childhood, this doesn't surprise us, we might even say that in this we can discern the movement of god's thumb, or rather finger, which moves out of justice whenever it does move and won't tolerate any other sort of movement. The institution did everything that could be done in Tjaž's case, it tried to raise him and because he was less susceptible to instruction and recalcitrant in his insistence on doing wrong, it devoted an enormous amount of time and care to him, we can safely say much more than to all the others, whom it consequently had to neglect, it gave him advice, shared useful life lessons with him, it tried by hook or by crook, in short, it did everything it could, not just so Tjaž could live, but live as befits any baptized individual, and if he were still alive now, you could ask him yourselves whether he adhered to those lessons, and if he didn't why he didn't, and so on, his wanton ways hardly made him rich, nor did they impoverish the institution, Tjaž remained the same person despite wanting to change, except that first he brought shame on himself, he fell to his knees to precisely the same extent that he tried to raise himself up, people are helpless and out in the world only rarely manage to find their way, particularly if their boarding school hasn't had sufficient opportunity to prepare them for it, the institution is not at fault for his death, he didn't learn that sort of thing here, we prevent things of that sort to the extent that it's in our power, we're not a funeral club or a cemetery society, the fault is entirely his, if you look at it the right way, because he didn't know how to help himself to the proper amount of freedom, here he got small portions, a bit at a time, just enough to leave you wanting the slightest bit more when it gets taken away, you feel satisfied and yet not satisfied, it's that little bit that's been withheld that makes you want more, it's administered in doses, so to speak, just big enough for a person to withstand without suffering ill effects, in the right amount then, the way god wants, but Tjaž stuffed himself full of freedom, there's no other way to refer to his stunts than with that ugly word, stuffed, and those were the reasons that he went to sleep with the fishes, he's sleeping with the fishes now, the way he deserved, all that stuffing made him overreach, he behaved like a pig with the feedbag, he wasn't up to life in freedom, he couldn't manage any moderation or restraint, so he saw his salvation in suicide, he thought it was the only way he could exculpate himself for his fickleness both in his own mind and in public opinion, undoubtedly he was influenced in that behavior by certain complexes having to do with his professional overextension, which must also be taken into account as a mitigating factor, we also gave him freedom of speech, of opinion, of thought, of decision, and of behavior in the form of the house rules, of course, there must be order, but within its boundaries all freedoms are possible, within that context he could permit himself the most contradictory interpretations of the precepts and regulations, all of which derive from Christian concern for our young people, this is well known, and which precisely for this reason are quite demanding for lukewarm Christians, we see this and take it into consideration to the extent possible, but in general more and more must be demanded so that a little bit can be achieved, you can see for yourselves the Christian spirit that emanates from all of the precepts and regulations of the house rules, as proof of that we quote the holy texts approved by the bishopric, this sort of verbatim quotation strikes us as the most appropriate manner of disseminating the house rules at first hand, in their untouched and unsullied—their virginal form, so to speak, as they have not heretofore been known to the wider public, and no one will be able to accuse us of having twisted them to our advantage, quite the opposite, this sort of text will lead anyone familiar with the subject to the conclusion that it would have been easy to abide by our rules and that those who didn't behaved with the utmost frivolity, it's hard to come to any other conclusion, you simply can't come to another conclusion in view of the risk of having the verbatim quotations distort the style and spoil the subtlety of our position, but for the sake of the thing one must simply assume the responsibility for such eventualities. Thus, the house rules very explicitly require that all residents of the boarding school must feel as though they belong to a single family—here begins the verbatim quotation—and thus each person must seek to uphold excellent interpersonal relations, just as god has instructed, and each resident is required to behave honestly in the boarding school and outside of it and to conscientiously observe the house rules, including all ad hoc regulations, on all occasions, and it is each student's obligation to study diligently and complete examinations in a timely way, and moreover to attend to his spiritual well-being, rank disregard of this duty may result in expulsion from the school, and owing to the risk of wasted time it is not permitted for anyone to linger in the room of another student for longer than ten minutes, numerous common rooms are available in cases where longer conversations are needed, explicit permission is required for group study in any private room, visits are permitted only in the ground floor rooms and only until 9:30 P.M., without special permission no one may bring anyone into the living quarters or host a guest other than his own parents in his room, and even in this case the school administration must be notified, female servants who reside at the school have free admittance to perform chores in the school offices only but shall otherwise have no admittance to spaces other than their own rooms, similarly the boys will have no admittance to employees' apartments and workrooms, order and cleanliness must be maintained in all rooms as well as the entire institution and care must be taken that nothing is damaged, all items of use must be left in their places in the reading rooms and common rooms, whoever is responsible for damage to school property must pay for repairs, if the name of the culprit is not revealed to the authorities then the costs of repairs will be assessed proportionally to all, under no circumstances are pictures to be nailed, taped, or pasted to the walls or furnishings, special permission must be requested to hang any decoration to the wall, a crucifix shall hang in each room and each student is required to rest his eyes upon their crucifix as frequently as possible, heed must be taken that electricity, gas, and water are not used in excess, a cord may be hung from screws over the washbasin, plastic hooks attached to the wall by adhesive or suction cause damage and are therefore forbidden, the quality of each student's residence at the school will depend on the extent to which he supports good behavior, therefore each student shall carry a copy of these regulations on his person at all times or else keep a copy in an accessible place, read them, and also meditate upon them, each student shall maintain a good reputation among his fellows both in and outside the house, defamation of the institution and its leadership is not permitted, each student shall take the utmost care not to make any noise at night, doors are to be closed very slowly so they do not slam, door handles are not to be suddenly released causing their lock mechanisms to clank, keys are to be turned slowly to prevent rattling, running is prohibited on stairs and in hallways, students should walk as quietly as possible, loud talking is unacceptable, each student is expected to sweep his room and dust its surfaces with a damp rag measuring 20 x 15 cm, waxed floors are to be walked on in slippers only, each item of clothing or paper must be in its proper place in each room, each Saturday the windows are to be cleaned with a damp rag and wiped down with newsprint, to air out a room it is generally sufficient to open the upper vent, each resident is responsible for any damage to drapes or window panes, in order to prevent excessive loss of heat in winter rooms are to be aired out only briefly, vents are to be adjusted very carefully to avoid damage, the use of refrigerators is limited to one special plastic container that costs thirty-nine schillings and one half-liter bottle, refrigerators may not ordinarily contain anything else, at this point we've reached the midpoint of our word-for-word quotation, each individual should have his own blanket upon which he may sit or lie, the school's blankets may not be used without sheets, pillows must be turned over for sleep to prevent soiling or wear, between pillow and sheets each student should have his own blanket or the equivalent, on the first Tuesday of each month each student is to leave his sheets on top of the bed and remove his pillowcase for the purposes of laundering, if the sheets have been soiled due to nocturnal seminal emissions those parts are to be tucked out of sight for the sake of the nuns who collect the sheets, care is to be taken in the washrooms before undressing to pull shut the plastic curtain, moreover to avoid wasting water the shower should not be left running too long or too forcefully, if some water splashes out of the shower the student should immediately wipe it up with a rag, after bathing each student should leave the washroom as clean as he would wish to find it, it is therefore to be cleaned with a sponge or a squeegee, with care to be taken that no hair is left clogging the drain, the same rule holds for the toilets, bottoms are to be wiped only with toilet paper, only the left hand is to be used when opening one's fly, the thing therein shall be taken out and held with three fingers of the left hand, the stream is to be aimed directly into the bowl and care taken not to let it splash, the last drops are to be shaken out by hand, no single piece of paper or drop of water may remain on the floor, while urinating one's eyes are to be fixed straight ahead, one is to stand upright and straight, each boarding school student is a straight and upright young man, we're still quoting word for word, visits to the toilet and washroom are also to be viewed as a part of each student's daily moral hygiene, because students are at such a great risk of impurity, their moral hygiene is to be regulated as strictly as possible: if you undress, touch, observe, look at, buy, or give someone or something away with lewd intentions, or if you write or draw anything lewd, or want to write or draw anything lewd, if you speak, sing, laugh, wink, hint, listen, or sniff lewdly, incite to or give cause for lewdness, or refuse to deter your neighbor from doing so, do not publicly resist it, if you think unclean thoughts, wish, long for, imagine, or do anything lewd or even just *want* to think, say, sing, laugh, wish, long for, imagine, look at, wink, hint, listen to, or sniff lewdly, or incite or give cause for lewdness, or do not deter your neighbor from it, do not resist it publicly, engage in impure acts alone or with others, no matter with whom, boy or girl, some older boy or some younger girl, with a boy or girl of whatever background, well-to-do or underprivileged, and wheth-

er the act succeeds or does not succeed, however many times and
however often, how long altogether and how long each time, and so
on—but remember: the acts necessary to purify the body, to ensure
bodily health, everything that happens to your body without your
wanting or being culpable for its happening, all of that is no sin, but
rather god's will, you see, such is god's will, in his infinite mercy god
created you like this, so show yourself worthy and follow good examples, turn out the lights, lights must not be left on needlessly,
smoking is prohibited, even adults are not permitted to smoke here
because the smoke blows into the chapel and Jesus can't stand smoking, if divine service is being performed in the chapel, no one may
disturb it with loud talking, if choral singing is heard in the hallways, whether the singing of a hymn, some refrains, folk songs, and
so on, these are to be listened to respectfully, divine service is god's
service, the television is turned on in the lobby from 7:30 to 10
P.M., important programs broadcast outside of this time range will
be announced on the bulletin board in the same place where the
schedule of the week's divine services—that is to say, holy mass—
gets tacked up, the television is not to be touched by anyone other
than the person authorized to touch it, you will not be allowed to
waste all of your leisure time watching television, each resident of
the school is obliged to contribute some of his free time to the needs
of the community, in summer for instance to picking blueberries in
the nearby parish woods, then back home to pick the fruit that we
press for juice and then sell, using the profits to reduce the cost of
tuition, each student must pick a certain amount of fruit for the
community, and whoever picks most will be publicly praised and
his name tacked up on the bulletin board, there must be order in
the picking of fruit, all should have a view to the common good,
picking should be exemplary and painstaking, no one may venture
more than one hundred meters away from the truck because it has
happened that some have strayed too far, disappeared in the bushes
and undergrowth, undressed there or not and had relations in the
brambles, or reached into each other's pockets and touched each
other until they defiled themselves, and this of course is forbidden

and bad for your health, therefore adherence to these rules will be strictly monitored, because there are so many women waiting in vain for a little semen, and all this toying around and squandering of it will no longer do, the school administration will no longer tolerate it, hence this restriction to one hundred meters, that far will have to suffice, blueberries in summer, as we've already said, and in autumn we harvest potatoes on some of the larger nearby farms, and if the farmers have daughters or other female helpers, they harvest in some other field or at some other time, and for this the farmers donate a few hundred pounds of potatoes to the school, then we must pray for the farmers that god give them a good harvest, and whenever we harvest potatoes on the margrave's land we have to be disciplined and precise in our harvesting because we have to be sure to make a good impression on his lordship, the margrave is an influential and respected man, we're slowly approaching the end of our word-for-word recitation of the house rules, whoever violates the house rules, even if just a single precept, will be required as punishment to write an essay on "The Christian Virtues of the House Rules," and whoever has already written that essay and violates the rules a second time and is required to write the essay a second time will be expelled from the school, two such essays are equivalent to expulsion, this Tjaž knew well, we have proof of that fact and here is Tjaž's handwritten essay on the Christian virtues of the house rules, we keep it with his other documents in the safe as a precious memento, yet even so he committed a second violation and the essay had to be written a second time, which, of course, he didn't do, nor did we force him to do it, he pronounced his own sentence, so his expulsion from the school was entirely legal, which is to say in accordance with the house rules, so as a result we had every right to expel him, he himself put the implements of justice in our hands. That he would end up like this a short time later is something nobody could have foreseen or even suspected, it's not what we intended, Tjaž just wasn't made for the institution and he stumbled more than walked in the door, he stayed here too long, we took him on account of his social status, out of Christian compassion so to say, he'd had no proper upbringing, no good examples, no respect, no ideals, and the fact of his parents' bad reputation, his father losing his job as a woodsman and becoming a drunken street sweeper, his mother sent to a camp for supporting the partisans, she shouldn't have done that, she brought all that nastiness and other nastinesses on herself, she infected the whole countryside, it was her own fault and she got what was coming to her, criminals have to be removed from human society so it can be protected from them, traitors must be eliminated, for those reasons we accepted him into the school, but his suicide has nothing whatever to do with the school, he never talked about suicide, never expounded suicidal thoughts, nor did his behavior give a suicidal impression, although he was a bit strange, whoever might try to somehow connect his suicide with the school would be going too far, a person like him simply couldn't end any other way than he did, he punished himself for straying onto the wrong path and finding himself unprepared to confront the senselessness of his own behavior, his conscience had been finely honed, in those few short years with god's help we managed to do that, and with a conscience like that he was able to see through his insignificance down to the finest detail, he got fed up with the boredom of his hollow existence from one day to the next and judged for himself—which is not to say that we approve the step he took, this we need to make crystal clear, absolutely not, even though we must admit that a certain amount of worry has dissipated along with his departure and we're free now of a certain responsibility, one worry and responsibility less, that's something that ought to be taken into account, yes, a certain burden has been lifted from us, man proposes and god disposes, man prepares and god delivers, man reaches and god touches, we carry a burden and stumble beneath it, and then he who is infinitely kind unburdens us, rolls one burden away from the others, the one we least expect him to roll away, but he does, we ourselves can't budge the heaviest burdens, but he just blows them away, all glory and honor to him for that, our people are not a faithful people for nothing, it was god's will that Tjaž die before he could cause even more harm, and he would have caused it most certainly, so it turned out best for everyone that he escaped in this way, may god judge him fairly, he didn't have much use in this world, we'll pray for the salvation of his soul, he'll need that, tomorrow we'll begin, because his guilt cries out to heaven, this really is a waste of ink and paper, because anyone could have foreseen that he would set himself against us, he cast a shadow over the institution, humiliated those of us who were his friends and who only wished him well, he skinned us alive and painted us black, but we forgive him, we didn't withdraw into a self-satisfied tower and surround ourselves with resentment, we didn't just throw him out of the school, we also forgave him, he cut off Malchus's ear, so to speak, and we healed it, he can't be without his ear, Malchus can't be without it and the ear can't be without Malchus, because the ear without Malchus isn't an ear and Malchus without his ear isn't Malchus, each thing should be paired up with its proper other thing, each thing should be in its proper place, we were always prepared to heal him if he came back, our fellow feeling and love for our neighbor kept us from excluding him once and for all, as by rights he deserved, not that we wouldn't have been ready to take him back in, who says that, we didn't obstruct his path, he could always have returned from out of the night into the implacable, bright light of day if he'd wanted, but he didn't, the institution is capable of some wonderful turns of phrase, the implacable, bright light of day, the words practically melt on your tongue, he didn't come back and he did come back, don't you see, that's the thing, he only came back enough for us to register his death and make the sign of the cross at the mention of his name, he didn't even properly greet us. We tried to patch over whatever could still be patched over, we went to sprinkle him with holy water, to pay our last respects, and now his obituary has been nailed to the bulletin board between the order of divine service and the schedule of TV shows both in remembrance and as a warning to everyone, his obituary is even on the church door which he used to pass through and by, people used to see him pass through or by there, but they won't see him coming to pass through or by there anymore, he passed through there and that's how he ended, because he didn't pass by with a pure heart and a spirit pleasing to god, and he didn't bow his head enough, those now are the fruits, those are the fruits, I tell you, the seed bag is empty and the harvest has begun, it's been overrun with weeds and there is nothing to harvest, because every stale food goes to seed, you weigh it in your hand but don't feel the weight, you weigh it and feel its lightness, the seed bag is empty and the harvest underway will not produce, it's a hopeless realization, it afflicts you and you leave, crushed and with the feeling that you're partly to blame for its failure, but you aren't, because you've done your duty, you watered and fed it, you pushed yourself and did everything you could, your back bending over time from the effort, but the earth didn't yield and that's that, you aren't at fault and there's nothing you can do about it, regarding Tjaž you have nothing to reproach yourself for, he got caught up in some love stories out there in the city and for that he had to perish, stories of a thoroughly worldly nature, thanks to their partial illegibility, unfulfilled love and the hidden nook where we found them, even his love letters point toward the café, as he lived, so did he die, god is just and makes no exceptions, apparently he didn't even shrink from the tendernesses that otherwise require the sanction of sacrament, and without the torments of doubt and temptation, which is to say deliberately, consciously and by plan he defiled another's body and his own, he befouled his soul, for shame, and then no confession, no remorse or firm resolution, no penance or mending his ways, it's unseemly, that's why he slept through all those holy masses and celebrations, the only things that keep a person on the straight and narrow, that's why the disruption of peace in the house, the house's compromised reputation and all the rest, in short, sin amid these walls that aren't made for sin, what would you do, it should have been nipped in the bud, but we couldn't take anything so scandalous as that upon ourselves, so it was only fitting for us to advise him to look for an apartment outside of the institution, he could even do a great deal of good on the outside, and anyway it would be better for him, that's how we argued it, but it was no use, because he refused to leave of his own free will and we had to remove him by force. Even though he had trumpeted so many ugly things about the institution, our deputy's homily at his open graveside was conciliatory, we went to great lengths to secure him a church burial, even though suicides generally don't enjoy that honor, but we succeeded in showing that he had committed his act in a state of spiritual blindness, so to speak, the doctor examined him and determined that his suicide had been the result of a physical disorder that had a negative effect on the psyche and vice versa, that the suicide was the result of mental anguish that had a negative effect on his physical state, more or less, and all of it during a full moon, that's what the autopsy revealed, and moreover let's be mindful of the sense of guilt that kept manifesting itself and burdening him, among his effects we discovered a diary that gives witness to a very modest intellectual life and a thoroughly dubious attitude toward the institution, and, you see, we also found a good deal of forbidden literature the titles of which—for pedagogical and publicity reasons—we can't enumerate here, but suffice it to say that we didn't find for instance any Thomas Aquinas or Thomas à Kempis, any Cyril of Alexandria, any Saints Augustine, Ambrose, Bonaventura, and so on, all those years he lived with us he was bizarre and unfathomable, this is true, his behavior was unusual and that whole routine of his with the fingernails, if we think about it, was simply baffling and really it was only a matter of time for him, in any case, so he was no longer responsible for his final actions, in short, they were the result of a mental eclipse, and on that basis we made a church funeral possible for him and we came out in full force to participate, so that we can rightfully call it a successful funeral, that gesture with the institution's banner when it dipped into the open grave made a huge impression on people—the institution bowing to its sons, most of the students dressed in black, a huge demonstration of sorrow, silence, and discipline, a funeral mass complete with leviticus, singing by the boarding school's choir, laments, the libera, speeches, a funeral repast, the divine office, in short a truly fine funeral the likes of which very few get to enjoy, the relatives were also informed, but they were aloof and preferred not to attend the funeral, as far as the school is aware, so it was the school that saved the day by turning out in force for the funeral service, producing a crowd and making the funeral a big success, a masculine and brief farewell, with less emotion than Christian bittersweetness, the oration was moving, based on the story of the nets with the fish, and how the kingdom of heaven is like a net cast into the sea that catches and fills with all different kinds of fish and then is pulled back onto shore, where they sit and put the good fish in a vessel and throw the bad ones away, we couldn't have done more for him, we are above reproach on that score.

I0.

A CHAPTER ABOUT
THE EARTH AND ALL OTHER EARTHS

On the day of the funeral it rained, if you will. From the very beginning, when I first took on this report about Tjaž, it was clear to me that Tjaž's story was not going to get past us without rain. If memory serves, at no place or time up to this point in our story has rain shown its irksome head, so it's time for it to do so now, while there's still a chance. And we'd better get moving, because the pitter-patter on the roofs is fast growing into a clatter, and a crowd of people has turned the street into a single black smudge, and their rushing about forces us to avoid the side streets and city squares, so we might as well have the procession take a shortcut and go through the park, that's the quickest way there. This chore was a nuisance for everyone, that much was clear, hence all the hiding, the dawdling, and the haste, come on now, let's go, into the ground with him, let's not waste any time. They head toward the graveyard in rabbit zigzags, avoiding the main streets and stores that are wrapping up their annual sales and just now stocking the new winter fashions, they say that prices are going up this year, so it's high time to turn on the rain, open up the sluices in the clouds and send down the fattest drops I can recall, if my memory serves me right, and god said let there be rain, and there was rain, the likes of which you don't see every day, and god set long, hard streams of rain against all those hats and holiday backs, a proper deluge dumped on them, a naked, prolonged rain without lightning or thunder, lashing away at them. Soon the houses were bobbing around in dirty puddles, they would get blurry whenever one of them bumped into another, a bell tower reached up out of the water's choppy surface, the cemetery got stuck in the mud, and we walked softly into the downpour, if you don't mind the poetry. I have to admit I was late and only joined the procession at the cemetery gate, I had various things to attend to, standing a little bit here and rummaging a little bit there, pausing a bit at a time, some little thing here and some detail there, all hardly worth mentioning, but little adds up into big and suddenly you're late and you catch up to the procession precisely at that moment when it's still a procession and not yet a crowd, so you've joined in at the last moment before its transformation, right before it dissolves and changes into a crowd that then covers the whole cemetery. Out in front is the bearer of the cross with a death's head mounted on a black pole that makes you shudder, behind him the children carrying lanterns, lots of young people, students from the boarding schools, a thoroughly organized funeral, somewhat fewer adults, which is unsurprising, it's not a good time, the autumn rush, preparations for winter, careers, jobs, work, grinding away, the rain and all that, an unimportant person in the coffin, one funeral they just can't make. The coffin shifts slightly on the shoulders of the arrhythmic procession of unschooled and inexpert pallbearers, novices, rank beginners at this trade. Tjaž and I were classmates, if you don't mind my personal involvement in the last chapter of this story, I joined in the steps of the funeral procession, whose orderliness in the course of those last few strides was already diffusing into the chaotic bustle of an anthill, and I was overcome with a sense of guilt, though I was unable to define it, to grasp its true shape, with trepidation I thought back to our school days together, which had barely produced a few modest shared highlights and contained woefully little of the obligatory compassion, empathy, and responsibility for one another, I recalled it so that the circumstances in which Tjaž was taking his final journey might appeal to him now, so that he'd finally sit up in his casket, take them in, and acknowledge their appeal, and have a look at the path that his pallbearers were walking. Most likely the pallbearers wouldn't even notice Tjaž sitting up in his casket, they would feel nothing more than a barely detectable restlessness on their shoulders and in the boards, a gathering and concentration of weight, a gentle and inexplicable shifting of weight from horizontal to vertical. Tjaž would rise up slowly and sit almost unnoticed, he would see the people following him two or three abreast, it's not at all exact and depends on the substance of their conversations, not everything is equally interesting to everyone, all of them with their eyes downcast, their heads boring holes in the street, and over those heads the casket on its way to the graveyard, its heavy railings creak on the pallbearers' shoulders, the rain tautens and smacks into their bodies, people step aside, they've decided that this procession isn't for them, it wends its way, heads bowed too low, under the wet treetops as a spiked wind dances around their ears and catches their clothes on its icy tips, driving grit into them one instant and rattling into the puddles the next. It's at this point that Tjaž notices me, and those leaden eyes blazing like coals threaten me and drive the last trace of our school years out of my soul. The part of town we'd reached, shoveling a path for ourselves through the storm, was one Tjaž knew by heart, so he would have got his bearings instantly, he would have registered the regional difference in the way the rain clattered, in other parts of town it clattered differently, the clatter of the rain would be all he'd need to know which part of town this was, nobody opens their windows as the funeral procession slinks past, people are used to scenes like this, it isn't the first or the last to play out under their eyes, the first one is like the next, and they're all alike, every last one, so they've stopped noticing them, they're far too modest to attract their attention, so the old craning of necks has become the exception, nobody gets up on tiptoe. Tjaž would embrace some things with his eyes, while others would get just a glance, he would stop at some places and walk past others, and he would remember quite a bit, he would remember the attic room where he had once been a guest, and the girl he'd grown entwined with, and if he looked closely, he would discover her now in the procession, but Tjaž doesn't look closely and he doesn't discover her in the procession, his eyes have served out their term, his pupils have seen enough, his heart has reached its quota and stopped beating, it's been recalled to the factory, his loving lips have worn out, the love that was shouted and preached from the rooftops has made a mockery of itself and imploded, stop making love, eat and devour each other instead, she's quiet and stares straight ahead as she tries to avoid the puddles, when the others pray, she doesn't pray, because she's not guilty, she sidesteps the puddles and those days of old appear before her eyes, how wonderful that they do that for her too and precisely at this time and place, what a convergence of way signs, what a harmony of two lives, days that she wasn't aware of before seem familiar and intimate to her now, she's aware of the greatness of those great facts, that he flickered to life beside her, that a human being burned out beside her, she understands the one who shut out everyone else in order to open up fully to her, today she would be strong enough to endure him without bounds or limitations, her virtues had been a sign of her immaturity, it wasn't from strength, but from weakness that she had shielded her breasts and defended her groin, she hadn't wasted or dissipated herself, he hadn't been able to put her on a leash, he hadn't been able to find her, but today he could have, she feels that, although it's too late, she's ready, because she's here and following the coffin, and the whole institution is here, but the institution is praying, even though it's not guilty, and all the others praying are here because they're righteous and they've prayed for so many before on this path, they're experienced and know what's fitting, all of them, from the first to the last, erstwhile advice-givers and know-betters, all-seers and chiders who've not had a moment's peace about her youth, they've complained about her age, that she's still so young and already chasing after a boy, she's even done *it* already, the impatient quail, and now she's done for, she's got a bun in the oven, they can't separate now, just imagine, she's done for, and at such a young age. They assessed her potential, bargained about her worth, haggled about her weight both live and slaughtered, felt over her back and her ribs with a butcher's precision to see how much meat was on them and how much fat, debated the ratio of meat to fat, which to be sure was not ideal, the day of slaughter was appointed, and after some hard bargaining about her worth and the cost they agreed on a price, the appraisers had finished their work and left the slaughter house, the results were announced, and after a bundle of polite words about the weather and requests to pass on greetings to family and friends the deal was settled, the poor creature was sold, and let's say that at the very end the sun came out or a slightly warmer breeze picked up, but today it rained by exception, we've already agreed to that and that's what we'll hold to, if you don't object. Sitting in the casket Tjaž would have been able to examine his legacy one more time and assess it, the chronological distance and the physical assimilation to the substances of the earth that began right after his fall to the sidewalk made this final review of his legacy possible. It turned out that he had done his work only halfway, he had been superficial, he hadn't mowed, just lopped off some stalks, the boarding school was blazing inside him, the unfinished work haunted him and he was just getting ready to rise up out of the evil past and get back on his feet, to grow up out of the casket and vault his slender body past all the frightened heads, he would pull himself up out of the casket, the lid would fly off, he would rise from the dead, to put it in your language, to the delight of some and the horror of others. While this temptation was rumbling in Tjaž's heart, the funeral director wasn't too comfortable with the situation, he couldn't stand to have Tjaž sitting up in his casket, much less leaping out of it. All funeral directors have a distaste for any theater that isn't prescribed by the liturgy and that isn't covered by that protocol, the reasons for this are obvious and are even plain for Tjaž to see, and that's why he doesn't sit up in his casket, but lies on his back and goes his way lying down and holds out this way, just as he's been instructed, he's late for the cemetery, and he himself recognizes that this whole process is taking far too long to complete, the funeral is behind, his death is wearing on people's nerves, and they'd better bury him as fast as they can, dig him in once and for all, for the sake of peace turn him to dust. There was one other event that day that made us think of the butcher's trade. We buried him right up against the cemetery wall, on the north edge of the cemetery, in case you're partial to that direction, beyond the wall there was a road or a railway or a cart trail that went by, from the start we weren't quite clear what was beyond the wall, and at last we decided in favor of a railway, because as they began to lower Tjaž into the pit, a locomotive peeked around the corner, luring a long series of cars behind it that were jammed full of cattle headed for slaughter a long way from here. At first the music of the rounded knives cutting into the rails, causing the steel to groan under the weight of the cows' bodies, stirred us to our very entrails, but then, level with the pit where we were depositing Tjaž, the cattle started to low, indiscriminately sending those low-pitched, harsh tones in our direction, why is unknown, perhaps the cattle were introducing themselves to us that way because they could see over the cemetery wall how the shovels were tiring of the mass of loamy earth. At the same time as the cattle, necks extended and tongues sticking out, held their low notes, another unprecedented thing happened—the cattle in the next car responded to the cattle in the first, and this dialog inspired all the other cattle, so that they started mooing in unison, the whole herd of cattle in all of the cars started mooing and lowing in all directions and for all they were worth, so that the hearts of all the butchers who heard it must have leapt into their mouths, the cattle speech echoed clearly through the cemetery and drowned out the dainty murmurs of the prayers, in one fell swoop it displaced the supplications, which couldn't have weighed much in the first place, or else they wouldn't have let themselves be driven out just like that, it put an end to the conversations in the rest of the cemetery, so that they had to be postponed to some other occasion and some later time, possibly even until the next funeral, the priest stopped his rituals, in an emergency there was no other way out, the altar boys were frozen in their black vestments and now seemed to sink even further into them, the vestments cinched even tighter around the ministrants' slender figures, they moved their chewing gum from the left to the right corner of their jaws, thus evacuating it to safety. The mourners turned around to look at the heads of the cattle that were craning out through the planks of the train cars and still hadn't stopped lowing, on the contrary it looked like they were just getting underway, their mournful, drawn-out, bitter cattle language wrung our hearts and saddened everything that had even the least bit of joy left in it, tears found their way to our throats, for the first time in my life beef soup with chives, parsley, pepper, Magi herbs, and leeks had such an effect on me, it was obvious to everyone that a lovely funeral had been ruined, and things began going south, the cattle's performance had been an introduction to further unpleasantness, and the old saying that all bad things come in threes proved itself once more, because shortly after the car with the cattle destined for slaughter passed out of sight and their moans grew fainter and then ceased completely, the casket started causing trouble. Whether it was too big and the grave was too small, whether the rain had warped the opening, or it too had been moved by the cattle lowing, or whether for reasons of its own the earth had clamped shut the muzzle that it had been holding wide open just a moment before, the gravediggers couldn't get it into the ditch, it resisted, it put up a fight whenever they attempted to commend the casket to its slimy grave, it refused to be persuaded, whether with kind words or harsh, they tried every possible means of submerging it, first from the front, then from the back, then turned over this way and turned over that, but all of it was in vain, all effort was useless, the skin on the backs of the gravediggers tautened, the muscles of their shoulders, their thighs and calves rippled, superhuman exertions were needed for them to turn it over and get it ready for the next position and next attempt, but they were no match for it one way or the other, whatever approach they might use, the casket refused to go into the pit as it should have, they couldn't get it to sink, and that was that, it was strange to look at the gravediggers doing battle with the earth over Tjaž's earthly remains, but the earth didn't want them, it wasn't interested. The priest began to fidget on the mound of fresh dirt, which was fine for his old feet in their new shoes, but other than that was pointless and meaningless, the shoes sank in from all his dismay, the altar boys shifted their chewing gum from upper jaw to lower, because they sensed that it was no longer in danger, and the people waited devoutly as always for what would come next, they were all patience, patience, just as the priest had taught them, it's on his account that they go to church, to funerals and weddings, it was for his sake that they carried banners and the canopy on Corpus Christi and Easter Sunday, because he's a good monseigneur and he has cancer of the pancreas, the disease had been visibly spreading, the danger was acute, the congregation had been seized with fear and concern for their priest, strong men forced their way to the front and stood ready, nervousness was spreading through the foremost rows and some women had started to cry and gnash their teeth, while the air was so swollen and thick with worry you could slice it. The gravediggers tried the only thing that was left—they turned the casket over, set it on its head, so that the corpse tumbled into the lid and flopped on its belly, its teeth biting into the wood of the lid, and behold, the effort succeeded. Greatly relieved we stood around the ditch that had now finally consumed Tjaž's boards, thank god there was one position it would agree to, the gravediggers wiped their brows, until now they had tried hero-ically to tame their responsibility and now they were rid of it, their joy was clearly written on their faces when they sent the thing head-first into the ditch, and if there was anything left to do, well, they would let the earth take responsibility for that. It would do its work without delay, you can be sure of that, first it would pull the boots off his feet, starting its work with the footwear, then it would pull the skin off his body, and a short while later it would relieve the tendons and muscles of their roles, deprive the joints and ankles of their functions, suck the meat off his bones and the juice from his marrow, leaving the marrow for last, never fear, the earth will take care of this, as is customary and right in these parts, the last scratch-ing that Tjaž will experience in this world will be the most thorough of all and will be aimed at him. We stood around the ditch in a halo, with kerchiefs on our heads and hats in our hands, with gum in our jaws and squishing in our teeth, one of those kerchiefs was Nini's, one of those hats belonged, for instance, to the owner of the skyscraper café, whom Tjaž's death had greatly distressed, one of those stumps exposed to the rain was the church bell tower, built to honor this or that saint at the expense of this or that nobleman, and with the participation of this or that person, and let it be noted here, one of those umbrellas may have belonged to some relative of Tjaž, who had meant to head for a pub or the market, but took a wrong turn and wandered into the cemetery just as it was witnessing the gravediggers' heroic efforts. Rain poured from the sky without mercy, the mourners conjured their umbrellas and swore at the water in their shoes, but the rain whistled uninterruptedly over the multitude of umbrellas, the umbrellas repulsed it, buried it, gave shelter, as the water fell over him, yes, the umbrellas poured hymns on him so that the burial wouldn't stick in its tracks but keep moving forward and come to an end, it's business as usual, manufacturing the product, achieving our goals, umbrellas move the ritual along, and if you can stand this repetition of umbrellas, the rain pitters on them relentlessly, and it drips from the larger umbrellas onto the smaller umbrellas, and from the smaller umbrellas it drips onto the ground, and onto people without umbrellas, the clothing of the mourners soaks up the rainwater, the rainwater sneers at the clothing and the clothing sneers at the rainwater, they pass the work back and forth, do their best for each other, refusing to be in each other's debt, if you will, of course the rainwater prevails as it sneers at the clothing and, moreover, deposits mud in certain places, with particular concentrations around the areas of the trouser cuffs, the fly, the sleeves and collar, after this work is over they will have to attack the mud with a special detergent, preferably one that's being advertised on the radio, this week that's dixan and omo, too bad this time for persil and henko. I've already stressed that we were standing around the grave in a halo and were blessing it for finally swallowing up Tjaž's coffin and rescuing us from an unpleasant situation, and let me call your attention to the word halo in this sentence. We stood in a halo and took the grave as our center, right next to the grave stood the one doing the burying, in other words the officiating priest with the title of municipal priest, to his left stood his technical support, to his right his liturgical and ritual team, and behind them a ring of nuns who are the quickest to appear for a funeral, and who only have to change black clothes for black and put on a ring that has the inscription "Christ savior of the world" engraved on it, which they normally keep in a special box in the medicine cabinet or on a nightstand, it varies from nun to nun, so a ring of nuns who are practically made for these occasions, and the public in back, usually ordinary mortal folk under the protection of countless umbrellas. I aligned myself with the mourners and I approached the umbrellas, in other words, I contributed my umbrella and engaged it with the rain for the time being, there was no other work, the umbrella agreed and expanded above me so I could attend the funeral festivities without a care. People began to stick to the walls of their clothing either because of the funeral and the lengthy, interminable standing around or because of my share among the other umbrellas, in other words, because I had contributed my umbrella to the other umbrellas unannounced or because of the onset of winter, I'll be damned if that matters, winter seemed a long way off, and it was looking a lot more like a late autumn than winter, it was still too early for winter, the trees were squeezing the last bits of warmth out of the ground, so you see, that's autumn, if you'll agree, a slippery fog was pitching its tents over the asphalt and sidewalks, and the tree branches were already crackling, as a result of which within several hours the first overcoats started appearing, all of them still smelling of mothballs, but winter was still far off and refused to be provoked by the irritant of mothballs. There was no doubt that people were getting ready for winter, but they were doing it in a way that suggested winter was letting nobody get too close yet. That day Tjaž was the only one who harbored no reservations about the winter and first frost, he had done his hard work and would no longer have to head out into the cold to do it, he was safe, taken care of. Right as the priest was approaching the high point of the burial, the first snowflakes slapped into his face, they sliced right into his creases, but I'm sure the good man didn't feel their sharp edges, for he was filled with the ritual, his office blazed

forth from his words and gestures, he praised the earth that at first
had resisted swallowing up Tjaž but that they had finally managed
to tame, tricked into submission just as they had successfully repulsed the lowing cattle, he exculpated it before the mourning
crowd, somewhere a bell in a tower rang to the rescue, and the
crowd, which was shivering with cold, started to murmur. I can't see
the speaker exactly and I can't understand what he's saying, because
I'm standing too far in the background and he's turned his back to
me, but his words still seem familiar, I must have heard them somewhere before, all I can hear is his homily voice, which the rain keeps
slapping to the ground, that's because of the distance, because I'm
way in the back, perhaps he looks like what I imagine, or perhaps
he looks different, the features of his face are perhaps angular here
and perhaps rounded there or the other way around, angular there
and rounded here, it really doesn't matter and it's his business anyway how he arranges his face. He's satisfied with the commas and
periods of his sentences, I can hear that from back here, he has no
problems with his voice, his memory works fine and bravely delivers the mixture of Tjaž's life details and Christian edification that he
studied the night before last, there's no shortage of saliva for the
time being, we'll see how things go later, the paragraphs take shape,
the thread running through them unspools and glints in every sentence, his speech is progressing marvelously. The man stands outside in the light from the windows of nearby buildings, the windows donate their light, before the speaker's eyes can use the light
they polish and shape it, as long as the speaker preaches, as long as
his umbrella wavers above him, beneath which an angry clapper
strikes a mute bell during the disastrous Easter procession, the
whole time the windows of the neighboring buildings have to provide light, the whole cemetery isn't up to it, it's raining in dark
sheets and the rain hardens the gloom on its cloud ceiling, it constantly bristles out of the clouds, so that the speaker with his voice
gets closer and closer to distilled water and farther and farther away
from the people, if there's any difference, that is. The light of the
neighboring windows falls on his face, his hand is tucked into his

coat pocket, lingering where it's warm and dark, which leaves more light for his face, and his right hand speaks of peace, joy, and reward. The umbrellas are the first to agree with the speaker's words. When it's raining and a person is shivering, when the rain rolls off the big umbrellas onto the smaller ones and from there onto the people without any umbrellas, that's when it's easiest to believe in joy and sunlight. In Tjaž's final seconds, when he was still conscious but had already begun to join up with the concrete-hard sidewalk below, he must have had a disgusting taste in his mouth, he must have regretted his decision, he died for himself down there, certainly not for any of the people who are crowding around his grave now, and that's why he could choose his own method, he didn't have to take anyone else into account, an ailing old mother, for instance, or the enterprising and indebted neighbor who always gave him milk but no longer would from now on, all he needed to find was the occasion, he died at his own discretion, with no reservations or excuses, from start to finish, from front to back, all in a row according to circumstances, and because he got there first, he caught the worm, the early bird catches the worm, and the earlier the bird, the better the worm it gets, the fuse burns down more intensely, he died from the top down, from the café down to the sidewalk he died, in other words straight, with no detours, upright, a boarding school student is upright and straight. We've arrived to see the ripening harvest, the eloquent bumbershoot of a speaker says, the trampled field has risen up from its barrenness and so forth, the grain has sent forth ripening ears and so on, washed by the rain it shows golden in the sun and so forth. Because I knew Tjaž and we were classmates, which may not be much, but is at least something if you like that sort of detail, then just by dint of our being classmates I knew that all those words were false, lies from the first to the last syllable. Tjaž never shone golden in the sun, he sped toward his destruction, everybody knew that, any kid on the street could have confirmed that, that alone is the truth and there's no need to conceal and ignore it just because it makes philistines uncomfortable. I have to give the speaker time to find a place to pause, so that the holy ghost can strike him down and together they can correct this error, now that the funeral has finally gotten going, only now come off, so to speak. I also have to give the mourners enough time for the burial, let them bury him, let them shove him into the grave and winter him there, at least until the bell tolls, people are standing around and contentedly tossing dirt into the grave, some from close up, others from a distance, they throw it and the dirt lands on Tjaž's back, where they've put him in teeth down, the four short legs of the casket jutting up in the air. I have to wait until enough dirt lands on Tjaž's back and between the casket's legs. The funeral is basically over, the participants have contributed their parts, the roles have been played, the mourners are content because they've gotten rid of the casket so cheaply, they've pulled out the hook that held neither fish nor bait, the ministrants have chewed their way through to a new pack of gum, the priest swung the incense and wished the deceased dust to dust, the choir cooed a lament for those present, who at the appointed moment resumed sniveling and wiping in no time, so after some initial disasters the funeral took a turn for a happier, more successful end after all. More time will be needed for shaping the grave mound, for putting out flowers, lighting candles, and setting down wreaths, so I'd rather not bother them while they're still hard at work, let them do a thorough job and let those expecting it be compensated, after all I suspect that digging a grave, shaping a mound, washing, dressing, and putting a corpse in a coffin all cost money, only the dirt that they throw after Tjaž is free. I have to give them time for all that, and the last of it to find a pub for the funeral feast, but despite the feast Tjaž's story doesn't end happily. I took on the story of Tjaž because it was thought I would be the most felicitous person for it, and not because it interested me personally, such is the bread of the reporter's profession, often coarse-grained with its crust slightly scorched, and that's precisely the reason I couldn't take it on with any enthusiasm, because my friends couldn't stop urging me to give them something funny, our people are a fun-loving people, conceived in laughter, born with a smile on their mothers' lips, they carry their burdens smiling and when they collapse beneath them, they give smiling thanks that they didn't collapse before now, and smiling they climb into their graves, for they don't like somber stories. Tjaž's story is a somber one, I knew in advance it wouldn't be fun. I broke it up into chapters and my heart was heavy. Tjaž the boarding school student stopped me and there was absolutely no fun shining out of his eyes, I sought out Tjaž the child and was stunned by the harshness of his first steps, I saw Tjaž making love and walked past, neither Tjaž the child nor Tjaž the man radiated any light or sun or peace, the way the lying speaker said at his open grave. Whichever one I chose and no matter how I approached him, there were always bitter thoughts that disturbed me. I remembered Tjaž the scratcher, but I would have the taste of wormwood in my mouth and my tongue would go limp with bitterness if I held to that memory. But you want funny stories, I'm supposed to provide you with laughter and jokes, you need entertainment and you're thirsty for fun, your lives are care-free—raising bees, solving crossword puzzles—I just regret I haven't been able to serve you better, you'll have to look elsewhere for your laughter and fun, you'll have to meet your vital needs some other way. I think the mourners have finished by now and that their work has been given the final seal of approval, I also think they've settled accounts and I haven't shorted anybody on time, I've left enough time for the cemetery to go bare and the people to disperse in every direction, the nuns have fluttered off on their gentle wings, even the priest has used the time well, after adding on a few final signs of the cross, he's sailed away with his entourage back to the sacristy and turned the space over to the mourners most intimate with the deceased, though there was no need really, because after he left the heap of fresh dirt remained all by itself, this time the grave mound was left standing vigil in a deserted space with no remaining mourners. The important bits are done and done: Tjaž is buried, the people feel relieved, they've found their peace and contentment, we've put him successfully under the sod, there wasn't a soul who didn't feel relieved and didn't walk away with the feeling that at the hour of greatest need he showed up and proved himself a man. It finished pouring, the clouds broke up, and as I closed my umbrella and began walking toward a patch of blue light, my eyes squinted over an empty burial site.

TRANSLATOR'S
NOTES

p. 17 *Peter Klepec*: the hero of a popular Slovenian folktale dating back to the sixteenth or seventeenth century. Klepec was a timid shepherd boy who became—thanks to the intervention of a fairy—strong enough to uproot trees with his bare hands and fend off the entire Turkish army.

p. 106 *Cankar, Župančič, Murn, Kette*: Ivan Cankar (1876–1918), Oton Župančič (1878–1949), Josip Murn (1879–1901), and Dragotin Kette (1876–1899) are Slovenia's canonical early modern writers.

p. 106 *Carantania*: the early medieval kingdom (or duchy) ruled by the earliest Slavs inhabiting the area of present-day Slovenia and Austrian Carinthia, beginning soon after their migration to the region from lands to the east in the seventh century. Carantania continued to exist as a more or less sovereign entity into the tenth century, at which time the Slovene lands were fully absorbed into the Holy Roman Empire and ruled by German nobility until the collapse of the Austro-Hungarian Empire in 1918. No sovereign Slovene political entity would exist again until 1991, when Slovenia declared its independence from socialist Yugoslavia.

FLORJAN LIPUŠ was born in 1937 in the village of Lobnik pri Železni Kapli (Lobnig near Bad Eisenkappel), in Austrian Carinthia. Since 1960 he has been one of the foremost proponents of Carinthian Slovene literature and its leading prose writer. He is the author of five novels and six book-length collections of short fiction and essays in Slovenian. In 2004, he was awarded the Prešeren Prize, Slovenia's most prestigious award for lifelong literary achievement.

MICHAEL BIGGINS's literary translations include the memoir *Necropolis* by Boris Pahor, the novels *Northern Lights* and *The Galley Slave* by Drago Jančar, Vladimir Bartol's *Alamut*, and numerous other books and shorter pieces from Slovenian and Russian. He lives in Seattle.

In 2010, the Slovenian Book Agency took a bold step toward solving the problem of how few literary works are now translated into English, initiating a program to provide financial support for a series dedicated to Slovenian literature at Dalkey Archive Press. Partially evolving from a relationship that Dalkey Archive and the Vilenica International Literary Festival had developed a few years previously, this program will go on to ensure that both classic and contemporary works from Slovenian are brought into English, while allowing the Press to undertake marketing efforts far exceeding what publishers can normally provide for works in translation.

Slovenia has always held a great reverence for literature, with the Slovenian national identity being forged through its fiction and poetry long before the foundation of the contemporary Republic: "It is precisely literature that has in some profound, subtle sense safeguarded the Slovenian community from the imperialistic appetites of stronger and more expansive nations in the region," writes critic Andrej Inkret. Never insular, Slovenian writing has long been in dialogue with the great movements of world literature, from the romantic to the experimental, seeing the literary not as distinct from the world, but as an integral means of perceiving and even amending it.

MICHAL AJVAZ, *The Golden Age.*
The Other City.
PIERRE ALBERT-BIROT, *Grabinoulor.*
YUZ ALESHKOVSKY, *Kangaroo.*
FELIPE ALFAU, *Chromos.*
Locos.
IVAN ÂNGELO, *The Celebration.*
The Tower of Glass.
ANTÓNIO LOBO ANTUNES, *Knowledge of Hell.*
The Splendor of Portugal.
ALAIN ARIAS-MISSON, *Theatre of Incest.*
JOHN ASHBERY AND JAMES SCHUYLER,
A Nest of Ninnies.
ROBERT ASHLEY, *Perfect Lives.*
GABRIELA AVIGUR-ROTEM, *Heatwave*
and Crazy Birds.
DJUNA BARNES, *Ladies Almanack.*
Ryder.
JOHN BARTH, *LETTERS.*
Sabbatical.
DONALD BARTHELME, *The King.*
Paradise.
SVETISLAV BASARA, *Chinese Letter.*
MIQUEL BAUÇÀ, *The Siege in the Room.*
RENÉ BELLETTO, *Dying.*
MAREK BIEŃCZYK, *Transparency.*
ANDREI BITOV, *Pushkin House.*
ANDREJ BLATNIK, *You Do Understand.*
LOUIS PAUL BOON, *Chapel Road.*
My Little War.
Summer in Termuren.
ROGER BOYLAN, *Killoyle.*
IGNÁCIO DE LOYOLA BRANDÃO,
Anonymous Celebrity.
Zero.
BONNIE BREMSER, *Troia: Mexican Memoirs.*
CHRISTINE BROOKE-ROSE, *Amalgamemnon.*
BRIGID BROPHY, *In Transit.*
GERALD L. BRUNS, *Modern Poetry and*
the Idea of Language.
GABRIELLE BURTON, *Heartbreak Hotel.*
MICHEL BUTOR, *Degrees.*
Mobile.
G. CABRERA INFANTE, *Infante's Inferno.*
Three Trapped Tigers.
JULIETA CAMPOS,
The Fear of Losing Eurydice.
ANNE CARSON, *Eros the Bittersweet.*
ORLY CASTEL-BLOOM, *Dolly City.*
LOUIS-FERDINAND CÉLINE, *Castle to Castle.*
Conversations with Professor Y.
London Bridge.
Normance.
North.
Rigadoon.
MARIE CHAIX, *The Laurels of Lake Constance.*
HUGO CHARTERIS, *The Tide Is Right.*
ERIC CHEVILLARD, *Demolishing Nisard.*
MARC CHOLODENKO, *Mordechai Schamz.*
JOSHUA COHEN, *Witz.*
EMILY HOLMES COLEMAN, *The Shutter*
of Snow.
ROBERT COOVER, *A Night at the Movies.*
STANLEY CRAWFORD, *Log of the S.S. The*
Mrs Unguentine.
Some Instructions to My Wife.
RENÉ CREVEL, *Putting My Foot in It.*
RALPH CUSACK, *Cadenza.*
NICHOLAS DELBANCO, *The Count of Concord.*
Sherbrookes.
NIGEL DENNIS, *Cards of Identity.*

PETER DIMOCK, *A Short Rhetoric for*
Leaving the Family.
ARIEL DORFMAN, *Konfidenz.*
COLEMAN DOWELL,
Island People.
Too Much Flesh and Jabez.
ARKADII DRAGOMOSHCHENKO, *Dust.*
RIKKI DUCORNET, *The Complete*
Butcher's Tales.
The Fountains of Neptune.
The Jade Cabinet.
Phosphor in Dreamland.
WILLIAM EASTLAKE, *The Bamboo Bed.*
Castle Keep.
Lyric of the Circle Heart.
JEAN ECHENOZ, *Chopin's Move.*
STANLEY ELKIN, *A Bad Man.*
Criers and Kibitzers, Kibitzers
and Criers.
The Dick Gibson Show.
The Franchiser.
The Living End.
Mrs. Ted Bliss.
FRANÇOIS EMMANUEL, *Invitation to a*
Voyage.
SALVADOR ESPRIU, *Ariadne in the*
Grotesque Labyrinth.
LESLIE A. FIEDLER, *Love and Death in*
the American Novel.
JUAN FILLOY, *Op Oloop.*
ANDY FITCH, *Pop Poetics.*
GUSTAVE FLAUBERT, *Bouvard and Pécuchet.*
KASS FLEISHER, *Talking out of School.*
FORD MADOX FORD,
The March of Literature.
JON FOSSE, *Aliss at the Fire.*
Melancholy.
MAX FRISCH, *I'm Not Stiller.*
Man in the Holocene.
CARLOS FUENTES, *Christopher Unborn.*
Distant Relations.
Terra Nostra.
Where the Air Is Clear.
TAKEHIKO FUKUNAGA, *Flowers of Grass.*
WILLIAM GADDIS, *J R.*
The Recognitions.
JANICE GALLOWAY, *Foreign Parts.*
The Trick Is to Keep Breathing.
WILLIAM H. GASS, *Cartesian Sonata*
and Other Novellas.
Finding a Form.
A Temple of Texts.
The Tunnel.
Willie Masters' Lonesome Wife.
GÉRARD GAVARRY, *Hoppla! 1 2 3.*
ETIENNE GILSON,
The Arts of the Beautiful.
Forms and Substances in the Arts.
C. S. GISCOMBE, *Giscome Road.*
Here.
DOUGLAS GLOVER, *Bad News of the Heart.*
WITOLD GOMBROWICZ,
A Kind of Testament.
PAULO EMÍLIO SALES GOMES, *P's Three*
Women.
GEORGI GOSPODINOV, *Natural Novel.*
JUAN GOYTISOLO, *Count Julian.*
Juan the Landless.
Makbara.
Marks of Identity.

SELECTED DALKEY ARCHIVE TITLES

HENRY GREEN, *Back.*
Blindness.
Concluding.
Doting.
Nothing.
JACK GREEN, *Fire the Bastards!*
JIŘÍ GRUŠA, *The Questionnaire.*
MELA HARTWIG, *Am I a Redundant Human Being?*
JOHN HAWKES, *The Passion Artist.*
Whistlejacket.
ELIZABETH HEIGHWAY, ED., *Contemporary Georgian Fiction.*
ALEKSANDAR HEMON, ED., *Best European Fiction.*
AIDAN HIGGINS, *Balcony of Europe.*
Blind Man's Bluff
Bornholm Night-Ferry.
Flotsam and Jetsam.
Langrishe, Go Down.
Scenes from a Receding Past.
KEIZO HINO, *Isle of Dreams.*
KAZUSHI HOSAKA, *Plainsong.*
ALDOUS HUXLEY, *Antic Hay.*
Crome Yellow.
Point Counter Point.
Those Barren Leaves.
Time Must Have a Stop.
NAOYUKI II, *The Shadow of a Blue Cat.*
GERT JONKE, *The Distant Sound.*
Geometric Regional Novel.
Homage to Czerny.
The System of Vienna.
JACQUES JOUET, *Mountain R.*
Savage.
Upstaged.
MIEKO KANAI, *The Word Book.*
YORAM KANIUK, *Life on Sandpaper.*
HUGH KENNER, *Flaubert.*
Joyce and Beckett: The Stoic Comedians.
Joyce's Voices.
DANILO KIŠ, *The Attic.*
Garden, Ashes.
The Lute and the Scars
Psalm 44.
A Tomb for Boris Davidovich.
ANITA KONKKA, *A Fool's Paradise.*
GEORGE KONRÁD, *The City Builder.*
TADEUSZ KONWICKI, *A Minor Apocalypse.*
The Polish Complex.
MENIS KOUMANDAREAS, *Koula.*
ELAINE KRAF, *The Princess of 72nd Street.*
JIM KRUSOE, *Iceland.*
AYŞE KULIN, *Farewell: A Mansion in Occupied Istanbul.*
EMILIO LASCANO TEGUI, *On Elegance While Sleeping.*
ERIC LAURRENT, *Do Not Touch.*
VIOLETTE LEDUC, *La Bâtarde.*
EDOUARD LEVÉ, *Autoportrait.*
Suicide.
MARIO LEVI, *Istanbul Was a Fairy Tale.*
DEBORAH LEVY, *Billy and Girl.*
JOSÉ LEZAMA LIMA, *Paradiso.*
ROSA LIKSOM, *Dark Paradise.*
OSMAN LINS, *Avalovara.*
The Queen of the Prisons of Greece.
ALF MAC LOCHLAINN, *The Corpus in the Library.*
Out of Focus.
RON LOEWINSOHN, *Magnetic Field(s).*
MINA LOY, *Stories and Essays of Mina Loy.*

D. KEITH MANO, *Take Five.*
MICHELINE AHARONIAN MARCOM, *The Mirror in the Well.*
BEN MARCUS, *The Age of Wire and String.*
WALLACE MARKFIELD, *Teitlebaum's Window.*
To an Early Grave.
DAVID MARKSON, *Reader's Block.*
Wittgenstein's Mistress.
CAROLE MASO, *AVA.*
LADISLAV MATEJKA AND KRYSTYNA POMORSKA, EDS., *Readings in Russian Poetics: Formalist and Structuralist Views.*
HARRY MATHEWS, *Cigarettes.*
The Conversions.
The Human Country: New and Collected Stories.
The Journalist.
My Life in CIA.
Singular Pleasures.
The Sinking of the Odradek Stadium.
Tlooth.
JOSEPH MCELROY, *Night Soul and Other Stories.*
ABDELWAHAB MEDDEB, *Talismano.*
GERHARD MEIER, *Isle of the Dead.*
HERMAN MELVILLE, *The Confidence-Man.*
AMANDA MICHALOPOULOU, *I'd Like.*
STEVEN MILLHAUSER, *The Barnum Museum.*
In the Penny Arcade.
RALPH J. MILLS, JR., *Essays on Poetry.*
MOMUS, *The Book of Jokes.*
CHRISTINE MONTALBETTI, *The Origin of Man.*
Western.
OLIVE MOORE, *Spleen.*
NICHOLAS MOSLEY, *Accident.*
Assassins.
Catastrophe Practice.
Experience and Religion.
A Garden of Trees.
Hopeful Monsters.
Imago Bird.
Impossible Object.
Inventing God.
Judith.
Look at the Dark.
Natalie Natalia.
Serpent.
Time at War.
WARREN MOTTE, *Fables of the Novel: French Fiction since 1990.*
Fiction Now: The French Novel in the 21st Century.
Oulipo: A Primer of Potential Literature.
GERALD MURNANE, *Barley Patch.*
Inland.
YVES NAVARRE, *Our Share of Time.*
Sweet Tooth.
DOROTHY NELSON, *In Night's City.*
Tar and Feathers.
ESHKOL NEVO, *Homesick.*
WILFRIDO D. NOLLEDO, *But for the Lovers.*
FLANN O'BRIEN, *At Swim-Two-Birds.*
The Best of Myles.
The Dalkey Archive.
The Hard Life.
The Poor Mouth.

SELECTED DALKEY ARCHIVE TITLES